CONTENTS

THE MYSTERIOUS DEATH OF THE DUKE

THE BALFOUR HOTEL BOOK 3

AMANDA DAVIS

Was the Duke of Holden's death a bizarre accident or murder?

James is obsessed with uncovering the truth about his father's untimely death.
Was it foul play?
If so, who is the murderer?
Or murderess?
Following a trail of clues leads him, his wife Lydia, and his mother-in-law to
The Balfour Hotel.

Lydia longs for passion in her marriage
Visiting the Balfour Hotel, surrounded by loving couples,
Only serves to pique her yearning...

...and, of course, there's Samuel, the handsome, attentive maître d'

As they frequent the halls of the Balfour Hotel,
Will Lydia find the romance she craves?
Will James learn who is responsible for his father's death?

Everyone's a suspect in this whodunnit.

PROLOGUE
EIGHT MONTHS PRIOR

I t was a still night, even for the late hour, and Byron stifled a yawn of boredom as his eyes traveled toward the door. He hoped that perhaps someone would venture through it. He yearned for some amusement to help pass the dismal night shift.

I am far too old for this roster, he thought with some misery. *I must speak with Samuel about switching my shift.*

He knew it would be a futile request. Young Matthew preferred his daytime schedule, and the Balfours seemed to favor Matthew, if only because of his pleasant face.

They will see me into an early retirement...or grave.

It was not quite the hour of two but, rather than risk falling asleep at his post, the elderly concierge rose to do his security rounds of the quiet, sleeping hotel. They were at full capacity. Even if a traveler happened into the lobby while he was on rounds, there were no rooms to give. Byron gathered the keys from the desk drawer to lock the front door before heading toward the staircase. With slow, laborious steps, he sauntered up the stairs from the lobby toward the second floor, his old bones creaking with the effort.

It was not a part of his duties that particularly appealed to him but he had been employed with the Balfours long enough to know they demanded nothing less than excellence. Tempting as it was to forsake the tedious rounds, Byron could only imagine what would occur if he were caught shirking his duties. After all, the Balfour Hotel was renowned through England for more than just its remote loveliness. The staff was always groomed, the service impeccable. It was not a job to be taken lightly but one which Byron cherished all the same.

As usual, there was not a peep to be heard on the second, third, or fourth floors of the hotel. The guest of the Balfour Hotel were of the highest caliber, of course. Rarely did incidents occur. And when they did, the Balfours managed to hide the would-be scandals with ease and decorum. It was merely one more of the numerous reasons why the Balfours and their establishment were regarded so highly.

When Byron stepped a weary foot onto the fifth floor, however, he was overcome with a strange sensation. The muscles in his neck tensed with apprehension. This was where the family lived and, inevitably, there might be some stirring of personal matters, regardless of the hour.

Matters had been unsettled since the abrupt disappearance of Mr. Xavier Balfour's new bride some months prior. While Byron did not know the specifics of Lady Elizabeth Balfour's vanishing, he *was*, unfortunately, privy to household gossip. From what he had gleaned, Lady Elizabeth had run off with her mother the very day after she and Mr. Xavier wed, and she had not been heard from since.

Byron did not put much stock in the rumors brought forth by the young waiters and chambermaids, but he did admit to himself that the situation was odd. Byron had seen the young couple together, and the adoration they seemed to feel for one another had been quite apparent. He had been just as stunned as the rest of the household by Lady Elizabeth's abrupt departure.

Since that fateful day, the tension, which always enshrouded the somewhat secretive Balfours, seemed to have escalated tenfold. It was no longer a matter of Mrs. Balfour stumbling from her chambers in a drunken stupor, nor the hints of raised voices, which Byron sometimes overheard as he padded through the halls. Overnight, it seemed there were open arguments between the Balfour men and Mr. Compton, the cries of baby Catherine, and the sobs of Mrs. Anne Balfour when she believed she was alone. The hour was irrelevant, and the friction was growing to insurmountable levels and felt by all.

That night, it was somewhat unsettlingly quiet on the family's floor, so much so that Byron paused to listen. Surely, the silence was a good thing, but Byron could not reconcile the stillness with contentment. In fact, the silence was downright unnerving, almost as though no one was behind the doors of the closed chambers. Of course, that could not be so. He had bid goodnight to all members of the Balfour family, including Mr. and Mrs. Elias Compton.

Could they finally be settling back into the way things were before Lady Elizabeth arrived?

Byron hoped for the best, but he could not help but sense that something was amiss—more so than usual that night despite the quiet.

None of this is your concern. Carry on with your business, a small voice urged him, and Byron forced his feet forward across the plush red runner of the corridor. He listened for any sign of life beyond the walls. As he reached the second set of stairs at the far end of the hall, he stopped again.

Through his peripheral vision, he saw a flash of movement. Before he could fully turn, whatever it was had already disappeared.

"Hello?" Byron called out in a muted voice. "Is anyone there?"

His words were met with only more silence. Byron's graying brows furrowed in confusion. He had been certain someone stood in the shadows, but as he retraced his steps, there was nothing of alarm to be seen.

I truly am too old for this shift, he grumbled to himself, again starting toward the stairs. He had wasted too much time on that floor and there was still the staff's quarters to be checked.

With quickening steps, he hurried along his route—only to be startled by a door slamming. Whipping about, his rheumy eyes widened and he gaped at the empty corridor. A shiver of fear raced down his spine.

I have always known there were ghosts in this hotel, he thought, his heart pounding loudly in his chest. *Now I have occasion to believe.*

"Hello?" he called again but now his voice was much lower, barely a croak. "Show yourself."

Nothing but silence. Byron decided he had had enough. Moving much faster than his brittle bones appreciated, he rushed to the staircase and began down the steps.

A shadow flew toward him in the dark, the flickering of candlelight drawing closer, and Byron froze in place.

I am being haunted for my sins. I was a terrible son. Mother, forgive me, he prayed, shutting his eyes as the figure closed the space between them. *Please, God, do not take me yet. I am not prepared to go!*

"Byron! What on God's earth are you doing standing there?"

His bloodshot eyes sprang open, and he exhaled with nervous relief as he recognized Joshua staring at him with surprise, a single candlestick in his hand.

"I was merely doing my rounds," he explained quickly, feeling foolish about his fright.

"Oh, thank the Lord," the young waiter sighed. "I thought I was taking leave of my senses."

Byron peered at the boy curiously, heart still racing loudly in his chest.

"Why is that?"

"I thought I saw someone leave through the front doors but that cannot be. You have the key to secure the entrance, do you not?"

"Yes, of course," Byron answered quickly, trying to recall if he had locked the front door. He was certain he had. He was nothing if not thorough.

The servants eyed one another until Joshua broke their uneasy gaze.

"Look at us," Joshua chuckled. "Frightening ourselves like small children. Is all well with the guests?"

"Yes," Byron replied quickly, brushing past the waiter toward his post in the lobby. Regardless of what he had told Joshua, he could not shake the feeling knotting his gut.

These nights will be the death of me, he mused.

As Byron stepped into the grand foyer of the hotel, he turned toward the front door to ensure it was secure. To his shock, he found it unlocked.

It was locked. I am certain.

Instinctively, he touched the pocket of his vest to feel for the keys. They were there. He chewed on his lower lip slowly, trying to make sense of who might have left.

The only others who have keys would be the family. Perhaps Mr. Balfour had pressing business to attend this evening. I did hear a door close. Yes, that must be what happened.

He willed himself to regain his composure, shamed at the idea he had let his imagination run amok. He did question what might call someone into the night so unexpectedly. Byron retreated to his post where he stayed, his back erect, his body unmoving, for the remainder of the night.

When dawn broke and Mr. Charlton Balfour appeared in the lobby by way of the stairs, dread again consumed Byron. No one had come in during the night, and Mr. Balfour was in the hotel.

"Good morning, Byron. How was the night?" the proprietor asked.

"Very good, sir," Byron replied. There was certainly no reason to bring up the peculiar instance of the previous night, not when there was no evidence that anything had happened at all.

"Will you send for a pot of tea before Matthew begins his time?" Charlton asked but before he could answer, the front doors opened with an authoritative gust of air.

The owner of the hotel and concierge gaped at the stiffly dressed man standing on the threshold.

A duchy guard, Byron thought. From which duchy, he could not be certain until the man strode forward and his crest became apparent.

He is from Holden. Has he news of Lady Elizabeth?

Byron's stomach flipped uneasily, and he had a terrible premonition of what was to come.

"I am in search of Lady Elizabeth Balfour," the guard stated, not an iota of warmth in his voice. "It is a matter of great urgency."

Byron looked nervously at his employer.

"Lady Elizabeth is not here," Charlton replied, stepping forward and saving Byron from a fumbling answer. "Who are you?"

"I must speak with Lady Elizabeth at once," the guard insisted.

"Then, I suggest you look elsewhere," Charlton growled, spinning back toward his office rudely. "Byron, my tea."

Byron stood nervously, his eyes darting back toward the guard who lost some of his sternness, replaced by confusion.

"I was told she had married one Mr. Xavier Balfour. Is this not the Balfour Hotel?"

"It is," Byron replied, and Charlton stood nearby, pretending not to listen. "But I assure you, sir, Lady Elizabeth is not here. She..." he faltered, unsure of what else to say.

"Oh, for heaven's sake. She has abandoned the marital home. She has not been here in months. What is the meaning of this?" Charlton barked, his face flushing as his own gaze darted about. He seemed concerned that guests might take notice of this out-of-place man in the lobby.

Shock colored the guard's expression.

"I-I was unaware of the circumstances," the guard muttered, looking abashed. "Forgive the intrusion."

He turned to leave but not before Charlton called out again.

"If she should happen to come about, what should I tell her?" the proprietor demanded. The guard paused. Byron read the uncertainty in his eyes.

"This is news that should be delivered personally to Lady Elizabeth," he insisted, but Byron could see him relenting where he stood.

"I am her father-in-law," Charlton snapped. "Out with it before my patience expires entirely."

Slowly, the man turned back to look at Charlton.

"Mr. Balfour, sir, it pains me very deeply to tell you this, but the Duke of Holden has passed."

Byron's eyes bugged slightly, but he knew better than to gape upon hearing the news.

"Passed? He has died?" Charlton demanded bluntly, and through his peripheral vision, Byron thought he saw a glimmer of pleasure light Charlton's face.

"Yes, sir."

"I see. How did this occur?"

The guardsman did not speak, apparently collecting his thoughts in proper order.

"It appears to have been an accident," he muttered, but even Byron's old ears caught doubt in his words.

"Indeed," Charlton muttered. Without hesitation, he turned away again. "I will relay the message if she should reappear. Good day."

Charlton then closed himself in his office, leaving the guard to bow awkwardly and continue on his way.

When Byron was alone in the foyer, his mind began to spin. He thought of the strange activity the previous night and the unlocked front door.

Could the duke's death be connected somehow?

Byron forced the terrible thoughts from his mind and hurried toward the kitchen to fetch his employer's tea.

If Charlton Balfour had some hand in this matter, it was certainly no business of Byron's. His loyalty was not to some duke he had never met. It was to the Balfours and their hotel.

1

Her mother turned up her nose in a deliberate fashion, scorn apparent on the woman's face. While Lady Elenora Blackwell had yet to speak her mind openly, her expression spoke volumes. Lydia was quite aware that it was only a matter of seconds before her mother's cutting words commenced.

With a white-gloved hand, Lady Blackwell ran her index finger along the sleek ivory of the piano and peered skeptically at it. From where Lydia stood, there was not a speck of dirt to be seen.

"The manor is certainly not well kept, is it?" Lady Blackwell sighed, forcing her daughter to smother a groan of discontent. It was not as though Lydia hadn't foreseen her mother's critique, but she had, perhaps naively, hoped for a pleasant visit. It was Elenora's first since Lydia had returned to Pinehaven with her husband, the newly appointed Duke of Holden.

"I have not had cause for complaint," Lydia replied softly, not wishing to be contrary, but she knew if she did not discourage her mother, the list of grievances would be endless.

"Perhaps I did not raise you to be as proper as I had hoped," Lady Blackwell sniffed, sliding through the parlor. "Or perhaps your standards have been lowered significantly already."

"Mother, please," Lydia begged. "These past months have been very trying for all involved. I would much rather we spend our time pleasantly."

The older woman cast her a dubious look.

"Would you rather I act as though I am pleased that you have left Whittaker to come to this monstrosity?"

"I would prefer that, yes, Mother," Lydia replied honestly. "Most ladies in your position would be quite enamored with the notion that their daughter has become a duchess."

Lady Blackwell scoffed.

"If they did not know the circumstances of how it had come to be," Lydia's mother conceded. "They might be elated for such a prestigious endowment. I, however, know better."

Lydia felt a smidgen of apprehension shiver through her.

"I do not know what you mean, Mother," she fibbed. "You know precisely how I came to be here."

Lady Blackwell scowled angrily.

"I will not fall victim to your plaintiveness, Lydia. You know from where my fears stem. Where is the dowager duchess? She has not stepped foot in Holden since the death of her husband, from what I have heard."

"Mother, you should not pay mind to active gossip. I daresay that is advice you have given me on many occasions."

"This is not merely gossip and you know it well!"

Lydia could read the indignation on Lady Blackwell's face, and she instantly regretted her words. Her intention had not been to further incense her mother but to ease her mind.

Alas, I should have realized that there is no reasoning with a suspicious mind.

"Mother, you must forsake this idea that the late duke's demise was anything but an unfortunate accident."

"An accident!" The contempt in the lady's voice was familiar.

"Mother, please!" Lydia begged her. "I do not wish to recount the sordid details of the late duke's passing. The matter still deeply troubles James."

"I would imagine so. His mother is likely responsible for what occurred."

"Mother!" Lydia snapped, her fair complexion waning as she looked covertly around to see if the servants were nearby. She did not wish for them to discuss Lady Blackwell's theory to her husband.

Not that it is a new one. The duchy has been alight with rumors and innuendo since the duke passed. The consensus is that the dowager duchess somehow had a hand in her husband's death.

"Fine," Lady Blackwell chirped, turning her head about to continue her scrutiny of the estate. She had only been there once prior, at Lydia's wedding to James.

She had been far more impressed then.

"I suppose it is a blessing that she has stayed away," Elenora continued, pausing to eye a painting over the mantel. "It would be detestable to know my daughter is sharing a roof with a murderess."

"Mother! I beg of you." Lydia's shock was lessening as Elenora relentlessly pushed the issue, but that did not put her mind at any ease.

She will invariably speak too freely before James and I will be in the midst of a terrible dispute.

There was little doubt in Lydia's mind that it would be a distressful fortnight. No amount of self-preparation would suffice. It was why it had taken so many months for Lydia to permit her mother a trip from Whittaker.

"Where is the duke?" Lady Blackwell asked as though she abruptly realized he was not there. "Has he no shame ignoring my arrival?"

"He is in London, Mother. I did forewarn you that he might not be here to receive you. He sends his apologies and assures me that he will be here on the morrow."

Elenora grunted in disapproval, and once more, Lydia found herself embarrassed by the lady's behavior.

"He has many duties now, Mother," Lydia reminded her. "Many more than he did as a marquis."

"Indeed," Elenora huffed. "I imagine that leaves little time for beginning a family."

She stops at nothing! If it is not one matter, it is another!

"Come, Mother," Lydia sighed. "You must be weary from your travels. I will have a bath drawn."

"I only just bathed," Elenora replied shortly. "I am quite well. If I have only a fortnight with my daughter, I would much rather spend it in her presence."

"Of course, Mother."

Lydia stood somewhat awkwardly, unsure of what else to say as Elenora continued her scathing tour of the parlor.

"Would you care for some tea?" she offered weakly. Suddenly, the walls of the room seemed to be closing in around her and breathing was becoming increasingly difficult.

Perhaps my corset it too taut.

Of course, she knew her breathlessness had little to do with her undergarments.

Lady Blackwell sniffed.

"I was wondering when you might ask," she said haughtily. "For such a grand manor, there are surprisingly few servants."

"They are about," Lydia protested. "I only asked that they give us some time."

In truth, she had asked them to keep their distance because she did not know what would fall from her mother's unbridled lips. There was more than enough gossip already without Elenora's contribution. No good adding falsehoods.

"I will find Ruth," Lydia said quickly, excusing herself.

"The servants should find you and not the reverse!" Elenora called after her, but Lydia paid her no mind as she hurried into the corridor leading to the foyer. To her shock, James stood just beyond the door, his brow scrunched in frustration.

"Oh, dear," Lydia sighed. "You are home."

"That was not quite the greeting I had expected, Lydia," he replied, but there was a little mirth in his tone.

"Forgive me, Your Grace. I simply had not expected you so soon."

"I hurried back from my interviews. I suspected that Lady Blackwell's company might be diverting."

Lydia did not wish to agree with her husband's astute observation, but she did not need to concede. James was hardly estranged to her mother's ways. They had, until recently, all lived in close proximity, after all.

"Did you overhear?" Lydia sighed and James sniggered.

"With all due respect to your mother, my darling Lydia, her voice does carry all the way to the gates. I daresay if I did not hear from here, I might have in London."

"Never you mind her," Lydia said quickly. "She is merely concerned about my welfare."

"And I am not?"

"James," she murmured, the knot of unease in her gut tightening. "We must do our best to ensure this visit goes smoothly."

James cast her a sidelong look, but he did not argue, to her great relief.

"How did your interviews fare?" Lydia asked brightly. "I was about to fetch some tea."

"I will require something much stronger than steeped water," James growled, and Lydia bowed her head.

"Of course, Your Grace. I will see to a proper drink at once."

"And I suppose I will see to your mother."

The words filled Lydia with dread, especially when her husband's dark eyes flashed with annoyance, but she did not stop him as she went to seek the servants.

We have endured much since returning to Holden, she thought with some sadness. *Mother could not have chosen a worse time to visit.*

Yet, as she made her way down the back hallway, Lydia realized that there might never be a good time for Elenora to visit.

The late duke's death had given Lydia some relief, a fact that she would never admit to anyone.

It was not only because the man had been a terrible brute, ill-tempered, and foul-mouthed. Lydia knew of his abusive ways, no

matter how James tended to turn the other cheek to his endless trans-
gressions.

When Mr. Balfour had come to Whittaker seeking James's sister,
Elizabeth, and their mother, Lydia had not been surprised in the least
that her in-laws had fled. In fact, a modicum of hope had sprung
inside Lydia. She had always feared that James's father might murder
his mother.

Yet that was only a part of why she had been sinfully elated to
learn of his passing. There was another cause for her guilty glee, one
which had to do with escaping the overbearing oppression of her
own parents in Whittaker.

Since she was a small girl, running through the grassy fields of
their small manor house, the earl and his wife had done little but
inflict their overly critical natures upon her. Lydia had not carried
herself well enough for her mother or been ladylike enough for her
father. It seemed it did not matter how hard she attempted to win
their favor; she could never do quite enough.

No one had been more stunned than Lydia when the Marquis of
Holden had proposed marriage. It had been one of arrangement, of
course, but James did not shy away from her, even in the presence of
comelier ladies. He was a decent husband, even for his short-temper,
which he had undoubtedly garnered from his father. He did not
drink or gamble like so many other noblemen Lydia knew of.
Certainly, James was a better man than her own father in many ways,
even if their connection was frigid.

Her hope had been that marriage would whisk her back to
Holden, but to her utter dismay, the earl had offered James a position
in his business. James had been quick to accept.

"But you are a marquis!" Lydia had gasped. "Your place is in the
duchy!"

"And you are my wife," he countered evenly, his eyes flashing with
anger. "You have sworn to obey me."

When the late duke died, James had little choice but to return to
Holden and claim the dukedom as required. James did not protest

the move, and Lydia knew then that her husband had only stayed in Whittaker to avoid his father.

Lydia had been certain that once they were on their own, their marriage would flourish and they might consider beginning a family. Some days, James seemed nothing more than a polite stranger, even if their short discussions were pleasant. In her dreams, she envisioned a romance blossoming between them, one where James saw her as a lady, one worthy of his affections. Instead, she was once more disappointed.

James seemed to retreat into himself even more when they arrived at Pinehaven, and Lydia saw less of him. They remained genial to one another, civil and proper, but they no longer shared a bedchamber. James had reclaimed his former rooms, and Lydia had taken over Elizabeth's quarters.

The nights were unbearably lonely, and Lydia did her best to occupy her days. If possible, she was even more desolate in Holden than she had been in Whittaker.

In six months, I am no closer to kindling a romance with my husband than I had been before.

There was only one thing for certain: having Lady Blackwell in Holden would do nothing to warm matters between her and James.

2

———

The manner in which Edward, James's father and the third Duke of Holden, had passed was not one that James took lightly. There had not been one moment since the new duke had learned of the strange circumstances that he did not suspect that something foul was afoot, regardless of how the house guards had determined the matter an accident.

How could a man simply fall to his death in a manor this size without being found for hours? Impaled on a statue, which should not have been there at all!

His hope had been that when he returned home to Holden with his bride, the situation would have become clearer. Instead, he found the case more puzzling than before.

This will drive me mad, he thought. *I cannot continue to pursue this matter when I have so many more responsibilities to attend to.*

Yet the reasoning did nothing to deter him from pondering the endless questions enshrouding the mysterious death. It did not help matters that he heard the talk in town, the flapping gums of the gossips who blatantly accused his mother of such an atrocious act, despite the lack of any evidence.

The dowager duchess's refusal to return to Holden only further roused the high suspicions. James secretly hoped that his mother, Patience, would have a change of heart and return to Holden now that his father was no longer a threat to her well-being. But her letters dictated that she was quite content in Luton.

He knew his wish was selfish. Patience returning would surely silence some of the more vocal busybodies in town, but James knew he could not force her to come home, not when she was with his sister Elizabeth.

Mother had no part in this atrocity and has no good reason to be in Holden, James assured himself, but he could not stop his mind from approaching the dreadful way his father had treated her and his sister. Still, he could not reconcile that the matriarch of his family had any such hand in Edward's terrible demise.

Perhaps if I had not gone to Whittaker, perhaps if I had remained, none of this would have happened.

James well knew he could not change the past. If Edward had not died, who knew where his mother and Lise might be today? Besides, all he had to consider were rumors and a mother-in-law with whom to contend.

Indeed, it would be a very long fortnight. James found himself resenting his wife somewhat for permitting Lady Blackwell's visit when his duties were still somewhat fresh.

Lydia is not to be faulted either. She does her best given the circumstances. It is Elenora who is deserving of my exasperation.

"Your Grace, have you disappeared entirely?" Elenora's sharp tone brought him back from his runaway thoughts and James forced a smile.

"Certainly not, my lady. I was merely considering some matters I need to attend in the duchy."

"Surely, they can wait while you are entertaining," Elenora retorted, some anger in her eyes. "You were aware of my arrival for several weeks."

"Sadly, Lady Blackwell, the duchy continues, even when embraced in the glow of your presence."

Elenora's mouth puckered into a frown, and she reached for her tea.

"Your flattery does nothing to appease me, Holden. Your charms will not distract me from what has happened within these walls."

"And what is that, Lady Blackwell?" James remarked dryly before taking a sip of his scotch. It was not a habit of his to imbibe, but the occasion certainly called for a disguising. He wished the alcohol godspeed at that moment for he was feeling much too clear headed for his own liking.

"Mother, please, do not start with such nonsense," Lydia begged. James had almost forgotten his wife was present as she hovered in the shadows, wringing her hands in nervous anticipation of what might occur.

What a dreadful woman to have to call your mother, James thought pityingly. *It is a small wonder Lydia has fared as well as she has.*

"You are entirely aware of what transpired here all those months ago," Elenora snapped, unperturbed by her daughter's pleas. "Your father, a great man, was murdered, and no one has been held responsible!"

Despite his determination to remain unfazed by his mother-in-law's brashness, James felt his muscles tense.

"I know of no such thing. The guards have determined it was a tragic misfortune, nothing more."

"And where were said guards on the night it occurred?"

"Mother!" Lydia was aghast, but James had expected as much. He cast Lydia a wary look, one which clearly read that his patience was already running thin with Lady Blackwell.

"It seems that you are privy to more information than I," the duke replied evenly. "Pray tell, my lady, what else do you know about that evening?"

His clipped words were not lost on Elenora, but she was not quite finished with her diatribe.

"I know that your father perished in a painful and most unpleasant manner, alone and unavenged!"

"I daresay, Lady Blackwell, it does sound as though you might have witnessed a crime."

Elenora balked and looked up quickly to meet his eyes.

"Me? Of course not. I was not here!" she sputtered, her face flushing red. Yet as the words left her surly lips, she seemed to understand James's point with clarity.

"You were not?" James demanded. "Then, how is it you know so much?"

Elenora's mouth parted, but no words escaped, and she quickly reached for her cup to cover the silence permeating through the salon. She would never admit that she was reiterating pure gossip.

"Mother, I suspect you are fatigued, regardless of what you claim," Lydia said, hurrying to escort her mother to her feet. "Why do you not rest before supper?"

"That is a fine idea," Elenora muttered, averting her gaze. James could see he had won that particular battle but there were undoubtedly more to come.

"Rest well," he told her nonchalantly, returning to his cups. He did not miss the apologetic look that Lydia gave, but he did not meet her eyes.

There was an unmistakable strain between them since they had arrived in Holden, one which James found regrettable, but he was unclear how to remedy the distance between them.

Our marriage is a matter for another time, he told himself, pushing aside the guilt building within him. *Lydia understands my distraction.*

Yet when they departed from the chamber, James could not stop Elenora's words from reverberating through his mind. She had merely fueled fears he had already had, even if her delivery was somewhat uncouth.

I will not rest easily until I know the truth about what has happened to Father, James thought, albeit not for the first time. *It plagues me terribly and affects every aspect of my life.*

The warmth of the alcohol spread through his body, slightly altering his already conflicted state of mind, and when Lydia returned to the salon, he stared at her with some blankness.

"Darling, you must not permit my mother to offend you," Lydia said without preamble, her gentle hazel eyes wide and worried.

"I do not," James assured her although he could not say if he was speaking the truth. "She only says what others have been thinking."

"This will pass. You must have patience, my husband."

She hurried to perch at his side on the settee, her nearness startling him some. It had been a long while since they had sat so close to one another, and James was stunned to realize how much he had missed her.

"I have nothing but patience," James answered, his eyes locking on hers. "But I cannot help but entertain her theories."

Lydia's brows raised slightly, and she exhaled in a rush of breath.

"James, you must not allow others to writhe their way into your mind. What happened to your father was a tragedy, nothing more."

"Was it?"

Surprise touched Lydia's face.

"Do not tell me you believe otherwise."

"I do not know what to believe," James admitted. "I do realize that this matter will not fade away as easily as I had hoped."

"James, you have interviewed the staff and spoken with the guards. The accounts remain the same. What doubts could you possibly have?"

"All of them," James said without hesitation. "I question every part of the tale and have since the night it occurred."

"Have you?"

"Yes," James replied slowly. "And I believe I finally understand why."

"Why is that?"

"I have not spoken with my mother nor sister about this, not at any great length. Their behavior was suspicious at best, criminal, if I permit my mind to go there. What they did to the Balfours, their disappearance...it is all quite suspect, is it not?"

"James, what are you saying?" Lydia breathed, wide eyed.

"I believe that my sister and mother know much more about what happened to my father than they have led me to believe."

"James, my mother has influenced your thoughts," Lydia cried, reaching for his hand in desperation. Her gloved fingers curled around him and she stared at him imploringly. "You cannot make such accusations without proof."

"I made no accusations," James snapped with some defensiveness. He knew that if he intended to pursue this matter, he might find answers he did not wish to learn.

But if I do not pursue this, I will never forgive myself. My father may not have been the kindest man, but he did not deserve a painful death. If Mother was somehow responsible...

He did not finish his own thought, but Lydia seemed to have read his mind.

"And what if you discover that Her Grace has done the unthinkable. What will you do then, James? Have her tried, executed?"

James's mouth became a fine line as his heart began to thud wildly in his chest.

"If she is responsible, she should be held properly accountable for her actions."

"Even after all your father did to her?" Lydia whispered, tears misting her eyes. James scowled and wrenched his hand back from her embrace.

"Nothing justifies murder!" he growled. "You almost sound as though you condone it!"

Lydia lowered her eyes to stare at her hands, the hurt evident on her face.

"I do not condone murder," she murmured. "But I did often wonder if your father would not have killed her first."

James's face flushed with indignation.

"He would never have done that!" he sputtered. "My father was a stern man, yes, but he would never have killed my mother!"

"If you say so, Your Grace." Lydia rose stiffly and smoothed the ruffles of her skirts, to keep her hands busy in her nervousness. "I will see about supper."

"Lydia," James called after her as she reached the threshold.

"Yes?" She turned with some reluctance, but she did not meet his eyes.

"I will not rest until I understand entirely what happened," he told her, his tone softening some. "It weighs heavily upon me."

Slowly, she raised her head to meet his gaze.

"I understand, but what else can you do in this matter? It has been six months. All the witnesses have been spoken to time and again. We have spoken to everyone."

James shook his head, his pulse quickening.

"No," he countered. "We have not."

She eyed him curiously.

"What do you propose, James?" she asked, a note of uncertainty creeping into her voice. He offered her a tight smile.

"I propose that you have the servants gather your mother's belongings and pack ours as well. I would like us all to leave for Luton on the morrow."

"Luton?" she echoed meekly. "My mother?"

James nodded curtly.

"If we are to get to the bottom of this mystery, we must interview my mother and sister. We shall go to the Balfour Hotel."

3

They took a coach and six to Luton, a journey that should have inspired some excitement in Lydia. The sprawling green landscapes were certainly ones that she normally would have adored along with the rhythmic clomping of the horses, but the duchess could feel nothing but anxiety as they traveled.

She had a terrible sense of foreboding as they closed the distance between Holden and Luton, her palms damp with distress, made worse by her mother's incessant complaining.

"Ridiculous!" Elenora sighed, her lips twisted into a sneer of disbelief. "I have no interest in spending time with a murderess and her daughter! I came to Holden to spend time with my own child!"

Through her peripheral vision, Lydia saw her husband tense although he did not say his thoughts aloud.

"Mother," Lydia said imploringly. "The Balfour Hotel is the finest hotel in all of London."

She deliberately avoided the topic of her own mother-in-law. She did not wish to consume her own words later if James's theory proved founded.

Imagine the scandal if Her Grace, Patience of Holden would be tried for murder!

It was something she could not bear to think about. James might never recover the respect of the duchy if it were learned he had permitted his father's death to go unavenged for so long.

It cannot be. I will not entertain this until I have seen proof in the matter.

"What if we arrive and there is no room for us?" Elenora continued. "What if—"

"That is quite enough, Lady Blackwell!"

Both ladies turned to James, shocked by his outburst, but Lydia was quietly surprised it had not come sooner.

"I beg your pardon!"

"I have heard nothing but endless quibbling from your lips since you arrived yesterday. I am the duke of the duchy, the head of the household, and I will not be questioned by an interloper!"

Lydia was stunned by his rudeness, but before either woman could get a word in, James continued.

"You have nothing but bile to spout from your lips. I have yet to hear one kind word spring from your mouth for me or my wife. You claim to have come to visit. It seems you have come only to cause friction."

Lydia's face flushed hotly and she looked away, but she could not deny the slight rush of pleasure that enveloped her body when she realized that he was speaking on her behalf.

He does care for me, even in his darkest hours.

At once, she was humiliated by her thoughts. James was worried about finding the truth and she was concerned about his feelings for her.

Childish. Indulgent, Lydia chided herself, but she could not stop herself from casting him a sidelong glance. To her chagrin, he was not looking at her but glaring defiantly at her mother.

"How dare you!" Elenora snapped. "My husband offered you a home in Whittaker, which you accepted without question. You have some gall accusing me of being unkind."

"Shrewish," James corrected, and before Lydia could contain it, a titter escaped her lips.

"You find this amusing, do you? He speaks wretchedly toward your mother and you laugh!" The disbelief on Elenora's face was enough to wipe the grin from Lydia's.

"Of course not, Mother," she mumbled. "Our wits are all frayed. This is hardly the time to squabble about trivialities."

"Harrumph," Elenora snorted, turning her head deliberately to stare out the coach window. Lydia raised her eyes to stare at her husband, and he shook his head, a bemused twinkle in his eye. Silently, she wondered how long he had wanted to speak his mind so clearly to her mother.

I imagine he endured just as much as I did while we lived with my parents in Whittaker. Father was not easy on him either.

The realization somehow made Lydia feel closer to James, but he had already shifted his gaze toward the windows, leaving her to feel somewhat lost in her place.

"There!" James called suddenly, and their attention trained on the stone structure which appeared in the distance. "That is the hotel."

Lydia's breath was briefly stolen as she stared the majestic white building. The grounds were as immaculately kept as any manor house she had ever known, the pathways groomed and tidy.

The scent of roses wafted through the carriage as the horses slowed upon their approach.

"I do wish you had sent word," Elenora could not resist muttering once more, but the couple paid her no mind.

"It is lovely," Lydia breathed, momentarily forgetting why they were there. "I daresay, I did not expect such beauty."

"I have been here only once before," James explained as the coach stopped, "with my father when I was a young boy. I confess, I did not remember it being so grand."

"I have seen grander," Elenora insisted, and Lydia stifled yet another sigh. There would be nothing that pleased her mother, that much was certain. She had long ago learned that. Why, then, did she hope that one day Elenora might soften her ways?

The coachman opened the door, and Elenora was the first to

alight. Lydia was still staring at the beautiful building, awed by its splendor.

"Lydia..."

She turned toward her husband.

"I had hoped that this trip would give you some reprieve from your mother," he said in a low tone. "Rather than leave the two of you alone at Pinehaven, I thought she might inflict her endless criticisms on others."

Lydia blinked. "I do not understand. What do you mean?"

"I would not have had you escort me on such an unpleasant task if your mother were not in Holden," he explained. A slow smile formed on her lips.

"I appreciate your concern, but you must not forget that I am your wife. There is nowhere else I belong than at your side, particularly during trying times."

James's eyes lightened, and he returned her smile.

"Perhaps," he murmured. "Would you object to sharing a bedchamber? I know we have not done so in many months."

Her heart sped at the notion, and she opened her mouth to answer as she nodded eagerly, but her words were cut off by Elenora's shrill tone.

"Must I stand in this heat alone? Such insolence!"

"We are coming, Lady Blackwell," James grunted with annoyance. He nodded for Lydia to move along, and she gathered her skirts in a gloved hand, reaching out with the other one for the coachman to take.

She stood at her mother's side in the blazing summer sunshine, blinking rapidly as her eyes adjusted to the blinding rays.

A bellhop appeared seemingly from nowhere.

"Good morrow," he said cordially. "Welcome to the Balfour Hotel. May I take your trunks?"

James appeared before either woman could reply.

"I request an audience with Mr. Xavier Balfour and his wife, Lady Elizabeth," James explained, and the young man's brow furrowed.

"Of course, sir. Are they expecting you?"

James seemed upset by the question.

"They are not." The bellhop was unruffled, his smile fixed firmly upon his face.

"In which case, may I tell him who calls?"

"James, Duke of Holden and brother of Lady Elizabeth."

The boy's lips parted as he took in James's formidable presence before dropping his head into a bow.

"Of course, Your Grace. Permit me to see you out of the heat, and I will seek out their whereabouts."

The bellhop wrangled the trunks, which the coachman had left upon the path, and struggled up the steps with the ladies close at heel.

The nervousness she had temporarily forsaken came flooding back as they entered the glorious foyer of the hotel. Despite being well dressed and of status, Lydia could not help but feel out of place.

Perhaps it is the intention behind our visit that makes me so uneasy.

She had little opportunity to consider her apprehension, though, as her mother stalked toward the concierge desk to rap rudely upon the counter.

"We will need rooms at once," Elenora snapped. "The best you have."

"Mother," Lydia breathed, joining her side. "Perhaps we should wait."

"Wait for what? The traveling has been hard on my bones." Elenora tapped against the counter again, and Lydia looked helplessly toward her husband, but James was focused on the grandeur surrounding them.

"Have you reservations, my lady?" the man behind the desk asked pleasantly.

"This is the Duchess of Holden, I am Lady Blackwell of Whittaker, and that there," Elenora pointed halfheartedly behind her, "is James, Duke of Holden, the brother-in-law of the proprietor."

"Mother..."

Humiliation flooded Lydia, and she wished she could disappear.

The concierge, however, seemed unperturbed by her mother's brashness.

"Welcome!" he said in a jovial tone, which Lydia was certain he reserved only for the most trying guests. "I will see what accommodations Mr. Xavier has arranged for you."

"James!"

The sound of a woman's voice caused both Lydia and her mother to spin as a very pregnant Lise Balfour shuffled awkwardly down the stairs, her face aglow with happy surprise.

"Lady Lise," he sighed, and Lydia witnessed the undeniable affection on his face. Regardless of their questionable upbringing, a sibling's love was forever.

"What brings you here?" Lise demanded, pausing to catch her breath on the landing. An abigail hovered nearby to assist her, but Lise waved the woman away. She smiled warmly at Lydia.

"And Lydia! As I live and breathe! What a wonderful surprise!"

"You look well," James said, stepping toward her and placing a hand on her arm, partially to steady her exhausted form but mostly in greeting.

"You always were a terrible fibber, James," she chuckled before rising to her full height. Her stomach protruded before her and Lydia guessed she had less than a month left before the arrival of their child.

A spark of jealousy seized Lydia, and she guiltily cast it aside.

You should be happy for her good fortune, not mourning your sterile marriage.

Still, she could not stop her longing gaze at Lise or wistful glance toward her husband.

"Oh, I cannot tell you how wonderful it is to see you," Lise gushed. "I must run and find Xavier."

"I would much rather see Mother," James replied, and Lydia's body grew rigid with dread.

He could not have waited a day? she thought but dared not speak her mind aloud. It was why he had come—to speak with Patience and learn what she knew about the incident that night, all those months ago.

"Mother?" Lise said, her smile faltering some. "Yes, of course."

She seemed to detect something in her brother's tone which she did not like but, rather than speak her mind, her gaze swung to Elenora.

"Lady Blackwell," she breathed, curtsying slightly. "Forgive me."

"Lady Elizabeth."

Elenora's tone was clipped, and she wore an almost disdainful look for the comely woman.

"Matthew," Lise called to the concierge. "Please find the duke, duchess, and Lady Blackwell a suite."

"At once, Lady Elizabeth."

"On the fifth floor," Lise continued. Matthew paused, his quill poised in midair over the roster.

"Yes, my lady." He quickly returned to his ledger without displaying any emotion.

They have learned not to question a thing.

"Why did you not send word that you were coming?" Lise wished to know. "We would have been well prepared for you."

"And ruin the element of surprise?" James replied dryly, but Lydia could see his eyes were clouded with guilt.

He does not enjoy lying to his sister.

"Where is your mother?" Elenora demanded quite unexpectedly, and Lise's smile froze upon her face.

"She is about. I will see you settled and then find her. We will have a lavish supper tonight in honor of your arrival," Lise continued, but Lydia could plainly see the concern on her face.

She suspects something already. Will she ask me the true nature of our visit?

Lydia swallowed the lump in her throat. She had no desire to fib to Lise, or anyone else for that matter, but her loyalty was to James, was it not?

"Well let us get on with it," Elenora grumbled. "I do not wish to stand here all day!"

"Of course, Lady Blackwell." Lise nodded toward the nearby bell-hop, and he reached for their trunks.

"Suites 505, 506, and 507," Matthew intoned, sliding the keys across the counter. Lydia's mouth formed a small O of surprise. Had she and James not agreed to share a bedchamber?

She looked at him expectantly, hoping that he would correct Matthew, but James was far too fixated on his sister to have noticed.

A sick feeling twisted Lydia's gut and she hung her head, defeated. She had naively thought that perhaps this trip would not be entirely abysmal, particularly if she might connect with her husband.

Foolish, silly girl. James has never seen you as more than an arranged bride. He does not much care where he sleeps. He was kind enough to ask you along so that you would not be alone with your mother, but that is all.

With a crushed and sinking heart, she followed the group up the curving staircase.

4

It was not until they were each secured in their chambers did James realize that he and Lydia had not been placed together.

Briefly, he considered remedying the arrangements, but he considered that Lydia had not mentioned the separation either.

Perhaps she did not truly wish to share a suite, after all.

That thought bothered him. Lydia was his wife, after all. She should be at his side.

"You will join us for supper," Lise told him from the doorway of the suite. "I will ensure everyone is present to greet you."

"Truly, Lise, I only wish to speak with Mother," James told her in a low tone. The abigail at Lise's side did not acknowledge him. The girl acted as if she was a deaf or mute, but James knew better. She was simply well trained.

"You will see Mother tonight," his sister replied. "She has spoken of you often these past months. I believe she was planning a visit to Holden soon."

"Does she need to plan a visit?" James scoffed. "It is barely a stone's throw away."

Lise peered at him speculatively.

"Why have you come, James?" she asked quietly. "And without announcement?"

"I cannot come to see my sister and mother?"

"Certainly, you can," Lise replied shortly. "But I have a rather uncomfortable feeling that you are here with ulterior motives."

James's eyes narrowed.

"What would you have me say, Lise? You and mother had all but forsaken Holden. It is not I who appears suspicious, is it?"

Lise balked.

"Suspicious, how?" Lise hissed, stepping into the room, uninvited. Without a word to the handmaiden, she closed the door, crossed her arms over her chest, and stared daggers at her brother.

"I meant nothing by it, Lise," he assured her, retracting his words quickly. He did not wish to cause friction between them without cause.

"You meant something," she insisted. "What is this truly about?"

"Lise, you and Mother have not been home since Father died. You sent for your belongings. You have barely sent letters. I have merely come to visit and ensure your safety."

"There is nothing in Holden for us but terrible memories," Lise sighed, her face softening some. "Perhaps it seems harsh, but Mother and I agreed that we would put the distance between us and start anew here. She is happy, James, for once. She smiles every day. Laughs, even! Can you ever recall a time when you have heard Mother's laughter?"

James pressed his lips together.

What does she have to laugh about? Her husband is dead! Is she laughing because she has gotten away with cold-blooded murder?

He did not express his burning questions aloud.

"I am pleased to hear that you are doing quite well."

"You must not forget," Lise continued as though he had not spoken, "I am about to give birth."

James cringed slightly at the reminder. It was hardly conversation in which he wished to engage, sister or not.

"Mother wishes to be close by for the joyous occasion."

"Of course," James said quickly, waving his hand in the air as though to dismiss the topic from his ears.

"And you?" Lise asked slyly. "You should be contemplating the start of a family soon, should you not?"

"I have more pressing matters to attend currently," James snapped with a defensive tone.

"What matters does Lydia have to attend? You have been married over three years. Surely, she is eager to start a family—"

"I do not wish to discuss my family affairs with you," James interjected curtly. "I would like to rest before supper, if you do not mind."

A fleeting look of hurt crossed over Lise's face, but she nodded in agreement.

"As you wish," she replied, opening the door and stepping back into the corridor where her abigail waited with the same blank, deaf-mute expression upon her face.

"Eight o'clock," Lise reminded her brother. "No later."

"Indeed."

The door closed, leaving James alone in the sitting room. He knew he should be thinking about what he might say to his mother when he saw her, but his mind was only on Lydia in the room to his left.

Lise is correct. Lydia has always wished to start a family. I wonder how she feels to know that my newly married sister is with child?

A pang of regret clutched James's heart.

She has been a most patient wife. She is not contrary or a spendthrift. Lydia has always run the household efficiently and gives generously to charities. She is a good wife. She deserves a child.

He vowed that they would start their family upon return to Holden.

That will please Lydia enormously.

∿

HE COULD NOT REST, despite his best attempts, and as the hour of eight neared, he found himself before the glass, fully dressed. Never had he been more dashing in a freshly pressed waistcoat of stunning midnight blue and matching ascot.

James could not say what it was that he found so particularly daunting. Was it seeing his mother for the first time in many months? Perhaps it was the idea of sharing more time with the ever-colicky Elenora Blackwell. Whatever the reason, James could not stop his gut from flipping with some discontent when he took his key and stepped into the corridor. To his surprise, Lydia waited in the hall.

"Lydia!" he called in surprise, taking in her lacy gown with undue interest. The swell of her bosom along the low neckline was breathtaking, her dark hair was piled into a stunning array of ringlets about her head.

"Oh!" she gasped, seeming equally as stunned to see him. "Forgive me, Your Grace. I was merely waiting on my mother."

Inexplicably, he felt a tinge of disappointment, although he could not say why.

Why would she be waiting on me?

"Of course. I will accompany you both to the dining hall."

"You need not. I realize how eager you must be to see your mother. We will be along when Mother has finished abusing the handmaid."

"If you are certain..."

"I am." Lydia offered him a smile, but it did not quite meet her eyes. "We will be along forthwith, I assure you."

James paused, feeling as though he should remain, but for what purpose? Elenora would most certainly put him in a foul mood by the time they reached the Balfours and Comptons for supper. He did not wish to be berated, not when his wits were already at end.

"Very well."

He turned to leave but not before he caught the look of wistfulness on Lydia's delicate features.

Did she wish for me to remain? If so, why did she not simply say so? Perhaps I had misinterpreted her look.

The fairer sex was rife with enigmas, which James did not claim to understand.

I certainly will not unravel them this evening, he thought bemused. Behind him, he heard a door open and Elenora's voice call out to snap at her daughter. This only caused James's feet to move faster, lest his mother-in-law insist he stay.

In moments, he'd arrived in the lobby. He barely noticed the guard until the elderly man called out to him from behind the counter, quite unexpectedly.

"Forgive me, Your Grace!"

James stopped, his eyes darting quickly toward the staircase.

"What is it?" he asked with some impatience. He was unaccustomed to being called upon by the help.

"My apologies, sir, but are you the new Duke of Holden?"

"I am. What is the meaning of this?" James demanded.

"I am Byron, the night concierge," he explained, but the introduction did nothing to alleviate James's mounting impatience with the man.

"What of it, Byron?" James insisted.

"I only wished to extend my condolences about your father," the man explained. James's eyes narrowed as he studied the concierge.

Is he ambitious or merely an idiot? Perhaps a touch of both.

It seemed odd that a man of such an age would attempt to curry favor with a duke, but his brazenness made little sense otherwise. James concluded he must be dim witted.

Servants are meant to be seen and not heard. To call out to me...that requires some gall. The staff is surely better trained than this!

"Did you know my father?" James asked curtly, his brows furrowing. Surely, this servant knew nothing of his father, but there was something desperate in the man that James did not understand.

Byron opened his mouth to respond, but before he managed a word, the irritating pitch of Elenora's voice interrupted their short conversation.

"There you are," Elenora grumbled insolently. "What are you bothering the desk boy about?"

James looked toward Byron, who no longer met his eyes and

pretended to busy himself with a flutter of pages. Whatever it was the old man meant to tell him was no longer on his mind.

"Nothing," James sighed, extending his arms for his wife and mother-in-law to take.

"Good. My stomach is causing a ruckus. When did we last eat?" Elenora complained.

"Mother, you ordered to your chambers not two hours past," Lydia reminded her as a doorman pulled the doors open to permit them entry into the dining room.

"It seems much longer. When one reaches a certain age, Lydia, one must insist on regular nourishment."

"Oh, Mother," Lydia sighed but James barely noticed their silly discussion, his attention was drawn to his own mother. With a some-what skittish look, Patience met her son's eyes, but it took her several seconds before she was able to smile at him.

"Ah!" Xavier Balfour rose as the trio approached, two other men following his example. "The guests of honor have arrived!"

James extended his hand toward his brother-in-law, and Xavier bowed as they touched.

"Your Grace, may I present my family. This is my father, Mr. Charlton Balfour, and his wife, my mother, Anne. Elias Compton and my sister, Emmeline. Of course, you know my wife and your mother."

James smiled pleasantly about the table before providing intro-ductions of his own.

"Charmed and pleased to meet your acquaintance. May I present my wife, Her Grace, the Duchess of Holden, and her gracious mother, Lady Elenora Blackwell of Whittaker."

Waiters stood by to extend chairs for the guests, and soon everyone was seated.

"Your Grace, we did send word when your father passed, but do permit me to offer my condolences in person," Charlton said, nodding to the waiters. Immediately, they stepped forward to pour wine as James maintained his composure. Through his peripheral vision, he noted his mother exchanging a look with his sister before returning her eyes to the plate before her.

"Thank you, Mr. Balfour. Your kind words are a great comfort."

"My kind words and a dukedom, I am sure," Charlton chortled.

"Have you no shame, Charlton?" Anne spat. "The boy lost his father."

James could not tell which he found more exceptional—being referred to as a boy or the idea that he would prefer the dukedom to his father's life.

"It was merely a jest, Anne. His Grace can plainly see that."

"It was not amusing in the least," Elenora snapped. "Particularly given the circumstances of the late duke's demise."

With wide eyes, James exchanged a look with Lydia, who seemed equally aghast by her mother's unbridled outburst.

"Mother," she breathed, but Charlton leaned forward, his eyes glittering with some interest.

"The terrible accident, you mean?" he asked, and Elenora snorted contemptuously.

"Hardly. I mean the murder, which Her Grace, the dowager duchess, likely committed."

5

The stunned silence that fell over the table was thicker than freshly churned butter, but it was quickly broken as Patience rose to her feet on trembling legs. Her hand flew to the coral necklace splayed about her neck, and she gaped openly at Elenora, who seemed unfazed by her blatant stare.

The men struggled to rise in unison as Patience threatened to storm from the table, but before she did, she turned her eyes toward her son and shook her head almost unperceivably.

"Is that why you have come, James?" she whispered, the surprise and disbelief in her voice causing a tremor in Lydia's heart. "To accuse me of murdering your father?"

"No!" James cried, also casting his mother-in-law a baleful look. "Of course not."

"He is simply too polite to say so," Elenora replied smugly.

Lydia hissed at her. "Mother, you must stop!" she pleaded, aghast. "What in God's name possessed you to say such a thing?"

Patience's eyes darted about the table, but she did not speak another word as she turned to scurry from the hall in a flutter of lace and silk.

"Mother!" Lise called, also rising clumsily, but her mother had already vanished, leaving the others to stare helplessly around the table in confusion.

"Lise," Xavier urged. "Please do sit. You should not be moving about so abruptly in your condition."

"I must go after her," Lise insisted as a waiter held her chair. She gave her brother a scathing stare before disappearing after Patience.

More silence ensued, and Lydia's face flushed crimson as she stared at the table in shame. Would God be merciful enough to open the floor and permit her to sink through it? She could not be so fortunate.

I knew this was a terrible notion, coming here, particularly with Mother.

"That is quite an accusation you make, Lady Blackwell," Xavier said, the anger in his voice apparent. "I do hope you have proof of such allegations."

"Do not be a fool, Mr. Xavier," Elenora retorted haughtily. "Surely, even you must have your suspicions about how matters unfolded."

"You are a spiteful, wicked woman!" It was Anne Balfour who spoke as she also rose, again causing the men to scramble to their feet. It was only then that Lydia realized that she was a trifle disguised. Anne's red-rimmed eyes narrowed dangerously as she fixed on Elenora.

"I cannot be faulted for speaking the truth," Elenora replied calmly, reaching indifferently for her cup of wine, but Lydia could see her mother's hand tremble slightly as she sipped, despite her intention to remain stoic.

"That is quite enough," James snapped. "No one is accusing Her Grace of anything. Lady Blackwell misspoke."

He glowered at Elenora, daring her to contradict his words, but to Lydia's great relief, her mother seemed to realize she was outnumbered.

"It does not seem that she misspoke," Charlton commented lightly. Of all at the table, he seemed the least upset by Elenora's claim. In fact, he almost seemed illuminated by the prospect.

"I should see to Catherine," Emmeline said suddenly, and in all the excitement, Lydia had almost forgotten that she and her husband Elias were present.

"I will join you," Elias agreed, and the couple also abandoned the table, leaving the remaining members of the unlikely family to stare uncomfortably at one another.

"I think it will suffice to say that our supper is ruined," Xavier snapped, but before he could rise, James called out to him.

"Please," he insisted, "do not leave on our account. We will retire."

"I have not eaten!" Elenora had the gall to protest, and all eyes widened dubiously at her.

"I will have something brought to your room, Mother," Lydia muttered, urging the woman to her feet. "Come along now."

Elenora pouted not unlike a petulant child. "I suppose I have no choice in the matter," she mumbled. "If the duke has spoken..."

"The duke has spoken," James agreed tensely. He looked at Lydia and she again hung her head in shame. She knew she could not control her mother's unstoppable tongue, but she had not expected such insolence in the presence of near-strangers, particularly not when they were guests of the Balfours.

"You need not go," Xavier said sternly, his eyes flashing. "I will see to my wife and mother-in-law."

He was gone before James could make another protest, and Charlton extended his hand, encouraging them to retake their seats.

"Now there is no reason for anyone else to leave," he said in a pleasant tone. "I do despise eating alone. Please. Stay."

Lydia gazed at James, who seemed nonplussed. Elenora, however, collapsed back into her chair without any further encouragement and reached for her goblet but not without giving Charlton a magnanimous smile.

"At last, a man with good sense and manners," she said.

"I do pride myself on both those qualities," Charlton chuckled. Lydia could barely disguise her disdain. The proprietor was enjoying the discomfort that her mother had caused.

"Do go on," Charlton insisted, waving for a waiter to pour more wine. "I would like very much to hear your thoughts on what happened to the late duke."

"She has nothing else to say on the matter, Mr. Balfour," James interjected as Elenora opened her mouth to speak. "Have you, Lady Blackwell?"

For the first time, Elenora met James's incensed eyes, and Lydia noted that she visibly swallowed.

"Indeed," she conceded. "I may have spoken too brashly."

"May have?" James barked. "You have caused an uproar based on nothing short of gossip!"

"Is there gossip?" Charlton wished to know. Lydia was somewhat appalled by his eagerness to discuss such rumors.

He is a renowned businessman. I would not have thought him one to entertain such nonsense!

Yet he leaned forward, his pupils dilated with interest as he waited for someone to speak. James put Lydia's innermost thoughts into words.

"I daresay, Mr. Balfour, I am surprised you are humoring such notions. I would think a man of your standing would have greater matters to attend than the inane tittering of the townsfolk."

Charlton pulled his eyes from Elenora to gaze steadfastly at James.

"Under normal circumstances, you would be correct," he conceded. "However, in this case, I find my curiosity piqued."

"As you should," Elenora agreed. "You may have a murderess living under your very nose!"

"I do wish you would stop saying that," James snapped.

"This is not merely about you, Your Grace," Lady Blackwell retorted. "This involves my daughter as well."

"Mother, I have no concerns," Lydia insisted, growing slightly dizzy from the conversation.

"I share Lady Blackwell's concerns," Charlton offered, and Lydia gaped at him.

"How can you say that?" Lydia demanded, forsaking decorum. "She has been a member of your household for months now!"

"I have heard quite enough of this nonsense," James growled, standing. "Come along, Duchess. I will not entertain another word on this matter until I have spoken with my mother."

"Run along, dear," Elenora chirped with too much smugness. "Be with your husband in his time of need. He will need the support when he is confronted with the truth."

Lydia did not wish to leave her mother unattended with Charlton Balfour. The way they looked at one another gave her chills, as though they were conspiring already.

"Lydia," James barked, and she reluctantly rose to her feet, her gentle eyes still warily set on her mother.

"Mother, do retire," she begged softly. "There is no need to further this tonight."

"Do not fret, Your Grace," Charlton told her genially. "I will see that your mother is safely returned to her chambers."

It was not Elenora's safety that worried Lydia at that moment, but she had no other recourse but to follow her husband from the dining hall as he fumed.

"Your mother is incorrigible!" he snapped as soon as they were out of earshot. "I should have known better than to bring her along."

"I am sorry, darling," Lydia murmured. "If I had suspected she would say anything so..."

"Vile? Bold? Disgusting?" James supplied and Lydia sighed.

"James, you cannot fault me for this," she implored him. "I would not have brought her along if not for your suggestion."

"Now this is my doing?" he demanded indignantly. "You have far more experience with her ways than I."

Defensiveness rose in Lydia, but she managed to keep her upset to herself.

How can he possibly blame me?

She did not remind him that he had lived under the very same roof as Elenora for three trying years.

"Never mind this now," James grumbled, spinning toward the staircase. "I must find my mother."

He did not wait to see if she was behind him as he hurried off, leaving her in the lobby, confused and upset by all that had occurred.

Perhaps Mother and I should return to Pinehaven, she thought, standing helplessly in the center of the lobby.

"May I assist you, Your Grace?"

A handsome man appeared before her, and Lydia startled at his unexpected arrival. He was an employee of the hotel, liveried and formal, with a sweeping mane of dark hair and a mysteriously dark expression.

"N-no," she managed. "I am well, thank you."

"Are you quite sure, madam? You seem...out of sorts."

He stared at her with warm, intelligent eyes, and Lydia felt a hot flush form beneath his intense stare. Despite his flawless English, Lydia wondered if he was perhaps of some foreign heritage, perhaps intertwined with the blood of moors.

What does he know about me? She wondered silently, but she could not bring herself to look away from the concerned expression on his face.

"If I were out of sorts," she breathed, attempting to muster some of her mother's arrogance, "I would certainly not be discussing it with a stranger."

He did not falter in the least, a fact that made Lydia respect him more somehow. Had he shied away, the illusion she was forming about this man would have evaporated into nothingness, and at that moment, he was the only thing giving her an iota of strength.

"I am Samuel, madam, the head maître d'. If there is anything you require, do not hesitate to ring for me—day or night."

His eyes lingered on her in such a way that made Lydia wonder if his meaning was not more subversive than they should be.

My word. You are looking to everyone with suspicion and hostility. This is not common of your character, Lydia. You must stop this at once.

"Thank you, Samuel," she murmured, breaking the eye contact between them. It was only then that she realized why the encounter made her so uncomfortable. A servant should not be meeting her eyes at all, least of all with such peculiar interest.

Perhaps they do things differently in Luton, she tried to tell herself as she nodded and moved away, careful to avoid his eyes. Lydia knew there was more to the seemingly casual encounter than she wished to admit.

As she stole back up the stairs in the shadows of darkness, she wished she had thought to light a candle but the encounter with Samuel had flustered her beyond logic.

You have taken complete leave of your senses, she determined when she arrived at her chambers. *On the morrow, you will discuss returning to Pinehaven with Mother and leave this place behind. Nothing good can come of being here. I should have had the good sense to foresee that.*

Yet, as she undressed to retire for the night, she could not get the image of Samuel's dashing face from her mind, and the idea of leaving seemed less appealing than it had at supper.

Ridiculous! Lydia chided herself furiously. *Off to bed with you.*

But sleep did not come easily to Lydia that night, and she spent several hours awake in the darkness, idly comparing Samuel to James and wondering if she was losing her mind.

6

J ames was not proud of the way he had spoken to his wife, but
he did nothing to remedy the situation. He was far too
consumed with finding his mother and making matters right
with her before Elenora's words did the damage she had
intended them to do. There would be time enough to speak with
Lydia later.

Unfortunately, he was unable to locate Patience anywhere in the
hotel, his unfamiliarity with the grounds much greater than his
mother's. He did chance upon Emmeline Compton at one point,
wandering the halls with her sleeping baby.

"Shh!" Emmeline begged. "I only just managed to get her to
sleep."

"Of course," James whispered, drawing nearer to inadvertently
steal a glance at the precious child. He was touched with a pang of
wistfulness as he stared longingly at the small girl.

"Catherine," he heard himself say. "A strong name."

"Indeed," Emmeline agreed, but James could sense she was
uncomfortable being in his presence at that hour of the night.

"Forgive me," he said, quickly collecting himself and drawing away with some embarrassment. "I am merely looking for Her Grace, my mother."

Emmeline studied his face closely, a shadow falling over her hazel eyes.

"Is that truly why you have come here?" she asked quietly. "To see your own mother hanged for the murder of your father?"

James was taken aback by the boldness of the question. It was enough that he was made to endure Elenora's shrewd tongue, but to be questioned by a woman he barely knew was another matter entirely.

He was a duke, not a servant. He commanded respect, not inquiries.

"Our family affairs are ours, Mrs. Compton," he snapped irritably. "I do not appreciate outsiders intervening."

To his complete surprise, Emmeline did not blink as she continued to rock her sleeping child.

"In which case, Your Grace, might I suggest you not air your affairs so publicly."

James gaped in shock, unaccustomed to being spoken to in such a blunt manner, but as the proprietor's daughter held his gaze, he realized that her point was quite valid.

Elenora did bring this upon us, he thought angrily. *She is the only one worthy of my annoyance.*

He nodded in concession and dropped his eyes humbly.

"I daresay you speak soundly," he agreed. "Forgive me."

Emmeline's face relaxed some and she also nodded, albeit curtly.

"If your mother did have something to do with your father's passing, I would hope you will not pursue it," she said, and James's head jerked upward, stunned again at her gall.

Does she know something about what happened?

"Despite what the countess has to say on the matter, I did not come here to accuse my mother of anything," James replied tersely.

"Then, Lady Blackwell speaks only for herself?"

"Mrs. Compton, you will forgive me if I would rather not discuss the sordid details of family matters in the corridor. I only wish to see my mother. Have you any idea where I might find her?"

Emmeline pursed her lips together as though she was considering whether to tell him.

"Her Grace, the dowager duchess, and my mother have become quite close over these past months," she finally offered. "I imagine that Her Grace has likely gone to my mother's chambers."

"Where might they be?"

It was Emmeline's opportunity to appear shocked.

"You cannot simply storm into my mother's chambers at this hour of the night," she said firmly, and humiliation flooded James's face.

"Of course not!" he scoffed like the idea had not even crossed his mind. "I-I merely wished to know for the future."

"May I suggest you return to your quarters, Your Grace, and rest. Matters might not seem so dramatic on the morrow."

James resented the advice, but he wisely held his tongue.

"What of my sister?" he asked, unwilling to release the matter until he had spoken at least to one of his kin. "Would she be with them?"

"I imagine, given Lady Elizabeth's condition, she would be sound asleep now."

James again felt a twinge of shame.

Coming here has only disrupted everyone. I should not have made this journey. On the morrow, we will leave.

"Of course," he rasped again, lowering his head further. "I believe I will heed your advice, Mrs. Compton, and retire for the night."

She cast him a half smile, which was full of an unspoken wisdom.

"Having unanswered questions about one's family can be daunting, Your Grace."

Slowly, James met her eyes again. Her words carried a deep wisdom.

"Yet I have found," Emmeline continued in a low voice, "that the truth always prevails in the end. You must simply have faith."

James felt his guard slowly drop as he absorbed her comments.

She speaks from experience, I gather. I wonder what secrets the Balfours have.

Quickly, he dismissed the idle thoughts. He had more than enough with which to occupy his time without delving into the affairs of other households.

"Thank you, Mrs. Compton. I bid you—and baby Catherine—a good night."

He bowed slightly as he spun on his heel and sauntered toward his own chambers, pausing outside of Lydia's door.

Briefly, he considered knocking, but he was once more confronted with the hour and decided to forsake the notion.

I will see her on the morrow, he thought.

～

A MANSERVANT APPEARED to help him dress the following morning, and James took advantage of it. He intended to make a good impression on the family after Elenora's gaffe the prior evening.

"Have you seen my wife, the duchess?" James asked the manservant, who held open a waistcoat for James to wear.

"Yes, Your Grace. She has already gone down for breakfast."

"With her mother?" James guessed, but Nicholas shook his head.

"No, sir. Or rather, she was alone when I last saw her."

James sighed, remembering the last words they had spoken. He had hoped to find her alone before Elenora ruined yet another gathering.

Perhaps if I hurry, I may still have a moment to have to speak privately with Lydia.

"Will there be anything else, sir?"

"That will do."

James cast himself one final look in the mirror before hurrying toward the door, where he paused to peer around the doorjamb and look down the hall.

Ridiculous. I am in hiding from Elenora.

Yet his own chiding did not stop him from checking a second time to ensure his mother-in-law was nowhere near.

With a long exhale, he scurried from his rooms and down the stairs toward the lobby, where he paused. His wife stood speaking closely with a waiter, oblivious to his arrival.

He watched, a peculiar sense of unease growing in the pit of his stomach as they continued their conversation. James could not say why the scene bothered him, but something inherent troubled him. Before he could make his presence known, Elenora arrived at her daughter's side.

Lydia whirled as though she had been struck, her face blushing pink at the sight of her mother, and James stifled a groan, his hesitation over the previous scene forgotten.

So much for approaching Lydia alone.

"Good morning, Your Grace."

He spun his head to see Xavier Balfour strolling down the stairs, a glint of anger in his emerald eyes.

"I trust your accommodations were adequate?"

"Yes. They were charming," James replied, hurrying after Xavier, who did not pause at his side but strode quickly past. It was clear the man was still upset about the night before, and James was determined to make matters right.

"Mr. Balfour, where might I find my sister this morning?" he asked and Xavier paused. Even without turning, James could tell he sported a scowl, but it was gone when Xavier turned to face him.

"She is resting in her room."

James's eyes widened.

"Is she unwell?" he demanded.

"She is with child," Xavier reminded him coldly. "And subject to the ailments of her condition such as fatigue."

"Of course."

He looked toward the stairs and then back to where his wife had stood moments. Lydia was gone, along with the waiter.

"Is there a matter with which I might assist you?" Xavier demanded.

"No," James said quickly. "Thank you."

"As you wish."

Xavier retreated toward the office and James turned toward the concierge desk where the young receptionist stood, pretending not to notice the friction happening in front of him.

"Where is the other man who mans this desk?" James asked, remembering the odd encounter he had shared with Byron.

"Sir?"

"The night guardsman," James said impatiently. "Has he retired, then?"

"He has. Shall I send for him?" Matthew asked, his brow raised. James shook his head.

"No need," he muttered. "I will find him later if I must."

"Very good, Your Grace. Is there another matter?"

"No," James replied as he decided what to do next. He very much needed to explain to his sister and mother that Elenora's words did not reflect his beliefs. Then, they would be on their way.

Yet he worried about what else Elenora might say in the dining room this morning if he was not there to keep her proper.

"Your Grace, do you need direction?" Matthew asked tentatively, and James considered that he needed more than mere direction.

"No," he said, realizing how conspicuous he must seem standing alone in the lobby, staring at nothing in particular.

I will speak with Lise and Mother before collecting Lydia and her blasted mother so we might return to Pinehaven this afternoon.

It was as good a plan as any, and he moved up the stairs toward the suite that Lise shared with her husband.

He knocked gently, feeling slightly guilty as he realized she might be asleep, but her voice called out for him to enter.

"Good morning, Lise."

She eyed him through the reflection of the glass with wary eyes as he entered the room and closed the door. She sat stroking her luxurious mane of dark hair with a silver brush, the handle gleaming almost as elegantly as her tresses.

She is radiant in her condition. I wonder if Lydia will be as beautiful.

He was somewhat surprised by the unexpected thought, but when he considered it, he realized that his wife had been weighing quite heavily on his mind.

"What is it, Jamie? Have you come to accuse me of killing father also?" Lise rasped at him, shattering his reverie.

"Do not speak nonsense," he grumbled at her. "Of course not. Lady Blackwell is a busybody who does not have the good sense to shut her impertinent mouth."

"She always was a bit brash," Lise conceded, but she did not manage a smile. "However, you must think me a fool to believe you came here merely as a social call without word or invitation."

"You are correct," James admitted. "I did come to speak with you and mother about what happened to father, but I realize now that it was a grave mistake. I will be on my way this afternoon."

A glimmer of irritation shone in Lise's expression, and her mouth tucked in at the corners.

"How could you suspect she would have anything to do with Father?" Lise demanded indignantly. "Why would we go through all we did to escape him if she had intended murder all along?"

"I...I am sorry, Lise," James offered lamely. "There are so many unanswered queries about that night—"

"Well, ask someone else about them!" Lise interrupted, her eyes flashing. "Mother could not have harmed him. We were leagues away, struggling for survival as mere peasants. I assure you, she had neither the means nor the opportunity to return to Holden. Not that she had any desire to do so. It took me an entire day to convince her to return after I told her of Father's death, James. She did not believe it."

Contrition filled him at Lise's impassioned speech.

"Of course," he sighed. "Mother could not. She does not possess a modicum of immorality."

"And yet here you are," Lise retorted. "Upsetting our lives after we had finally managed to put the unpleasantness of Holden in the past."

"I assure you, my dear sister, I will not pursue this matter again. Please, be well and write me when the child arrives."

I will go home now and focus only on my own, living family, Elenora Blackwell be damned.

Lise's mouth parted to respond, but as she rose to address him, her face contorted in a terrible expression of pain.

"Lise? Lise!" he cried as she stumbled forward, clutching her belly. Her face turned ghastly pale, and James's heart began to race.

"Come along," he insisted, supporting her quivering body as she moaned. "I will send for the midwife."

As they took their first step, Lise screamed out, the sound sending gooseflesh to prickle his arms.

"N-no!" Lise choked, tears of terror flooding her eyes as she clung to him. James embraced her tightly and peered at her in confusion. "Not the midwife!"

"Why?" he demanded. "Is it the baby…"

The sound of water caused his eyes to travel down along the lines of her gown, and his alarm grew into disturbed panic.

Blood stained her clothes, and James knew something was terribly amiss.

"N-not the midwife," she repeated, her voice growing weaker. "T-t-he surgeon…"

James stared in horror as his beloved sister went limp in his arms.

7

S amuel stood inconspicuously near the entryway, and Lydia could not stop herself from casting him several furtive glances when she was certain her mother was not looking.

She had been surprised to find him waiting for her in the lobby that morning, even if his presence caused her heart to patter dangerously.

"Good morning, Your Grace," he said, humbly bowing. "I hope you will not deem me insolent, but I did wish to ensure you had a pleasant night after your rather unpleasant evening."

Lydia knew she should not encourage his unwarranted attention, but she could not help but feel flattered that he had taken a moment to inquire about how she fared. Of course, she did not mention that her thoughts had wandered to him as she tried to fall asleep.

"I am well, Samuel. Thank you for your concern."

"I am pleased to hear it."

Their eyes met, and Lydia was sure she had never been as warm as she was in that moment. If not for her mother's arrival, she might have spent the entire morning in that very spot, melting beneath the maître d's gaze.

"My word, Lydia, at what are you gawking?" Elenora snapped,

bringing Lydia abruptly back to the present, and she quickly, guiltily, wrenched her stare back to her mother.

"Pardon? Oh, nothing," she babbled, fixing her eyes on the table. They were the only two at the family table to arrive, and she wondered if that had been by design.

We have only just arrived and we are already outcasts here.

Even as she thought it, the Comptons appeared at the threshold, and they ambled, arm-in-arm, toward Lydia and her mother.

"Good morning, Your Grace, Lady Blackwell," Emmeline called sweetly. "I trust you are well rested?"

"Indeed," Lydia agreed, casting her mother a warning glance. She hoped that Elenora had learned her lesson from the previous night, but who could possibly know what might spring from the Countess' mouth?

"I am pleased to hear it," Emmeline said as she and her husband joined the table. "Perhaps today we might enjoy a meal in peace."

Embarrassment touched Lydia's cheeks, but there was no mockery in Emmeline's tone, and the owner's daughter smiled warmly at the duchess.

"Where is His Grace this morning?" Elias asked as Samuel approached the table, distracting Lydia from the question. She could not stop herself from trying to catch his eye.

For shame! she thought, mortified at her reaction to the waiter's nearness. *You are a married duchess!*

"Your Grace?"

Humiliated, Lydia raised her eyes, certain her face was a deep crimson. She hoped that Samuel would not see her embarrassment, and that thought only shamed her further.

We must leave this place at once. You have lost your mind entirely.

"Pardon me, Mr. Compton?" she mumbled, struggling to find her voice and composure simultaneously.

"His Grace, the duke. Has he joined us yet this morning?"

"Oh…" Lydia steeled herself from giving Samuel another covert look. "I have yet to see him this morning."

She did not miss the quick exchange of glances between the

Comptons, as though they shared an unspoken message. Lydia had no doubt what thought they shared. They were unmistakably questioning why the duke and duchess slept apart.

How intimately they look at one another. Surely, they have never slept apart a day in their union. They have married for love, not like James and me. Moreover, they are blessed with a child and likely have plans for more.

She wondered what it would be like to be in a marriage where everything came so naturally, without work or feigned politeness. Certainly, it was not commonplace, but it did happen.

Not to ladies like me. I was meant to be at the side of a man who all but ignores me. My only hope for the future is in the children I hope to one day bear.

Again, Lydia shot Samuel a covert look. She wondered what it might be like to love someone who loved her back.

For it certainly seems like James will never be that man, despite how I long for requited affection.

"Will you be in Luton a while?" Emmeline asked brightly, apparently sensing Lydia's discontent. "There is much to do in the summer months, and I fear that I have lost my companion in Lady Elizabeth in her condition. It would be my pleasure to take you into the towns."

"No," Lydia said quickly. "We will be leaving forthwith."

She did not know what led her to make such a bold announcement without first consulting her husband. The table gaped at her in surprise.

"Forthwith?" Elenora demanded, and Lydia cringed inwardly. "We have only just arrived!"

If you had not spoken with such freeness, Mother, we might not be in a grand rush to leave, Lydia thought but, of course, did not speak the words aloud.

"There are matters to attend to in the duchy," Lydia lied. "Matters that cannot wait."

"What a pity!" Emmeline said, and Lydia saw that she was genuinely upset at the discovery. "I was rather smitten with the notion of a family reunion."

"Perhaps on our next visit," Lydia offered as Elenora snorted.

"I will not be back. I despise being carted about like cattle, Lydia. Whose idea was it to leave?"

"Mother, I implore you to mind your tongue this morning," Lydia growled in a low voice, quite uncharacteristic of her meekness. "You have done quite enough damage in a few short hours."

Elenora's face clearly depicted shock at her daughter's cutting remarks, but to her credit, she finally did hold her tongue.

"Where is Xavier this morning?" Elias asked, looking perplexed as he noticed the clock. "I saw your father in the office, Emmeline, but your mother and the duchess?"

He glanced apologetically at Lydia.

"Pardon me, Your Grace—I meant the dowager duchess."

Lydia could not be offended by the misappropriated title. She and Patience had spent so little time together that it was hardly a matter of concern. Still, she found herself wondering the same thing.

Where is James? Has he confronted his mother? Is that why they have not arrived?

"Perhaps I will see to my husband," Lydia offered, rising from her chair, but Emmeline shook her head at Lydia and placed her hand on Elias's arm as he stood to see her off.

"That is hardly necessary. I would very much like to enjoy a meal with you, Your Grace. The others will be along, I am sure. If you are to leave soon, surely you cannot fault me for wishing to spend our fleeting time together."

A burst of affection toward Emmeline ignited in Lydia, and she was overjoyed that she might find a friend in the seemingly cold hotel.

Possibly two friends, she thought, her mind on Samuel.

"Of course," she murmured, having difficulty subduing the excited smile that insisted on forming. "Forgive me for being so thoughtless."

"On the contrary, Your Grace. I notice you consistently putting the needs of others ahead of yourself," Emmeline offered softly.

"Darling..." Elias said in a slightly warning tone, but Emmeline maintained a soft smile on her face, her eyes fixed on Lydia.

"There is no harm in enjoying one meal without your husband, Your Grace," she continued, and Elenora snorted rudely.

"Particularly if that husband has no regard for others," Lydia's mother conceded.

"I am certain that—" Lydia started to say, but Emmeline raised her hand.

"There is no need to fashion excuses on anyone's behalf," she insisted. "This is the Balfour Hotel, after all. It is a place for a holiday, an escape from the cruelness of the world—if only for a short while."

Lydia tucked in her lower lip, carefully nibbling on the skin inside her mouth.

Perhaps we might stay another day or two, she thought hopefully. *I have never been away. James and I did not even have a honeymoon after our wedding.*

There was a sharp sensation in her chest as she thought about it. She and James might have used this time at the Balfour as an escape to discover one another properly as man and wife. They might have tried to begin a family or, at the very least, learned about one another as people the way Lydia had always secretly hoped they would. Instead, he was off on a chase for a murderer who might not exist.

She did not know why the fact hurt her. She had known for years that she was nothing more than his dutiful wife. Perhaps it was seeing the way the Comptons interacted or Xavier's anger toward James following Elenora's announcement at dinner.

This is how husbands are meant to behave with their wives, not ignoring them and dragging them about like a trunk or hat case.

"Duchess, are you well?" Emmeline called out across the table. "You have gone a lighter shade of pale."

"I am well," Lydia assured her, straightening her back elegantly.

"I imagine she is merely starving," Elenora commented dryly. "We have not had a morsel to eat in days!"

"Then, we must rectify that at once," Elias replied smoothly, ignoring the blatant hyperbole and signaling the waiters.

Suddenly, the double doors flew open with an unceremonious crash, and all eyes turned toward the threshold in surprise.

"Xavier!" Emmeline called, rising to her feet at once. "What is the meaning of this?"

Lydia watched, a surge of dread threatening to choke her as Xavier strode toward them.

"It is Lise," he croaked. "Something is terribly wrong!"

Waves of dread swept over Lydia, and she jumped to her feet, her mind awhirl.

"With the baby?" she whispered.

"Sit down, child," Elenora growled. "This matter does not pertain to you."

She did pay mind to the irony of her meddling mother's statement.

"Have you sent for the midwife?" Emmeline demanded, and Xavier nodded, wide eyed and pale with fear.

"And the surgeon. They are with her now."

Slowly, Xavier turned, a terrible anger replacing his panic as his gaze rested on Lydia.

"You must go collect your husband," Xavier hissed. The words sent chills through Lydia's body.

"W-where is he?" Lydia asked meekly. "What has happened?"

"I cannot say for certain," Xavier glowered. "But Lise was perfectly well before she was alone with him."

The insinuation stunned Lydia to her core.

"He would never!" she gasped, a hand flying to her mouth, but Xavier did not falter.

"I suggest you go for him before I do," Xavier insisted, and Lydia started blindly for the door, tears filling her eyes.

"Your Grace!" Xavier yelled after her, attracting all eyes in the dining room. Begrudgingly, Lydia turned back to him warily.

"Yes, Mr. Balfour?" she breathed, her voice barely a squeak.

"Perhaps you did not need to travel so far from Holden to find out who murdered your father, after all."

"Xavier!" Emmeline and Elias cried in unison, but Lydia did not respond. Instead, she ran from the hall to find her husband, wishing she could escape the doubts that Xavier's words had caused her.

8

James paced outside the bedchambers, worry plaguing him as the surgeon, midwife, and his mother remained inside the room with his sister.

Did my being here overly upset her? If I had not been here, would this have happened still?

It was impossible to know, of course, and when he saw his wife hurrying toward him, he exhaled with relief.

"Oh, Lydia!" he called, rushing to meet her. "My sister—"

"I heard," she told him quickly. "But we must not stay here in the halls, James."

He stared at her in confusion.

"I must wait on word. Her own husband has abandoned her. Someone must wait."

"Mr. Xavier has not abandoned her," Lydia replied, and he noticed a note of anger in her tone. "He has asked me to collect you, for he does not trust himself in your presence."

James blinked dubiously, certain he had misunderstood Lydia.

"I am the one who was here for her!" he cried, and Lydia gave him a scathing look.

"Lower your tone," she hissed at him. James barely recognized the woman before him. "We will discuss it in your chambers."

She moved toward his rooms, and he thought to argue but seemed to think better of it when he caught Lydia's scathing look.

"At once, James. We must not antagonize the others more than we already have."

"I did nothing," he insisted but followed his wife, shaking his head in disbelief. "How can he think I would harm my own sister?"

Lydia did not respond until they were inside the suite, the door closed firmly behind them.

"What happened? Why were you alone with her?" Lydia demanded, her questions fiery and pointed.

He looked at her in surprise.

"Not you, too?" he snapped. "I am your husband. How can you believe I would hurt my own flesh?"

"I did not say you did anything," Lydia countered, her face softening slightly. "I am merely attempting to make sense of what has happened."

She did not meet his eyes, and James was awash with worry.

"Lydia," he growled, approaching her to place his hands over her shoulders. "Look at me."

Reluctantly, she did as she was told and met his eyes.

"She is simply having complications with the child. I did nothing to harm her."

"Perhaps not with your hands," Lydia conceded. "But what did you say to her?"

"Nothing! I assure you, our discussion was civil. In fact," he inhaled deeply to steady the rush of words fumbling from his lips, "I told her we would be leaving this very afternoon."

Lydia eyed him uncertainly.

"You lied to her?"

"I did not," James sighed. "I had every intention of leaving the hotel this very day. Lise and I spoke about Father's death and how my mother could not have been responsible for his passing. I believed her, Lydia. I realized how ridiculous I have been these past months, consumed by this notion of my father being murdered merely because people like your mother have nothing better to do than flap their gums incessantly."

He paused again and lowered his hands along the sleeves of Lydia's dress, his eyes boring into hers.

"Coming here was a mistake—the way we did, bringing your mother..."

"Indeed," Lydia agreed, her skepticism seemed to be fading.

"I told her we would leave and she rose to embrace me, but then she doubled over. There was nothing untoward, I assure you. You must free your mind of such a terrible thought."

"She will tell Mr. Xavier the same when she wakes?" Lydia asked quietly and James bristled.

"You do not believe me!" he huffed, hurt by her question. "I am your husband!"

He could see that his argument did not sway her in the least, and he exhaled with a groan of frustration. Not that he could entirely fault her—after all, they were married in nothing more than name. How well did his wife truly know him?

It was a sickening realization, one that caused him great shame.

"Lydia," he murmured, his hands still firmly about her upper arms. "Perhaps we have not been as intimate as we should, but you must know at the core, I am a good, decent man."

She nodded but looked away.

"Of course, I know that," she murmured. "I would not have agreed to our union if I had thought otherwise."

He exhaled with relief.

"We should never have come," he continued. "The blame is mine alone, but we will return to Holden once there is word of Lise's recovery."

"Let us pray that there is," Lydia said with a certain flatness that chilled his heart.

"She is strong. Lise has always been strong. She and her child will prevail."

He did not believe his own words, but he had faith that God

would save her. James shuddered at the memory of his sister's limp body, the ghastly gray of her pallor as though death had come knocking for her right before his very eyes.

Two soft hands cupped his face, and he stared down at his wife worriedly.

"I cannot stand idly by, Lydia," he told her hoarsely. "I must know what has happened."

"You remain here," Lydia told him firmly. "I will see if there is word on Lise, but you must promise not to leave, James. Mr. Xavier is certainly out for your head, and I fear he will not heed any reasoning. Why, his temper might match yours."

James scoffed.

"I have no temper!" he insisted, and Lydia cast him a small smirk.

"Swear to me you will go nowhere," she demanded, and with a reluctant sigh, he agreed.

"But you must return the moment there is any word on my sister," he begged. Nodding, Lydia lowered her hands, but not before James seized them, his heart swelling with gratitude.

I have taken her for granted. She is good and kind, and I have been oblivious to her charms since the day we wed. I will not permit myself to be so foolish again.

"Thank you," he told her gruffly and watched her expressive face tinge pink.

"I am your wife," she said with some stiffness. "It is my duty."

She moved toward the door, leaving James with a heavy feeling in his heart as he watched her go. He could not suppress the feeling that he may have somehow lost her.

If I ever had her at all.

"Lydia!"

"Yes, Your Grace?"

She met his eyes, a shadow still clouding them to his chagrin, but she did hold his gaze.

"I had hoped..." he cleared his throat, and she waited, her head slightly tilted in expectation.

"Yes?"

"I had hoped that once we return to Holden, we might begin our own family."

A fusion of emotions played over Lydia's face, each one as fleeting as the next, and James was unsure how she felt about what he had said.

"Lydia?" he urged when she did not speak, a sense of dread growing in his gut. "What say you?"

"Of course, darling," she murmured. "That would be lovely."

Without another word, she disappeared from the rooms, and James was vastly unsettled.

It was a peculiar feeling, being left alone in the strange bedchamber, locked away like he was a prisoner. There was a helplessness to the situation that he had never felt before, and it was more than unnerving.

He paced about like a caged tiger and waited as the sun rose higher into the summer sky, the walls closing in around him with stifling heat.

What could possibly be taking so long? It could only mean something terrible had happened, he was certain.

To make matters worse, he still had not made amends with his mother, who had gone to tend to his ailing sister without so much as a word exchanged between them.

He thought of the promise he had made Lydia to not leave his room, but the anticipation was burning a terrible hole in his gut.

I must poke my head through over the threshold at the very least, he reasoned. *See if I cannot attract the attention of a—*

He cut his own thought off as his eyes rested upon the room service bell, and he almost laughed at his foolishness.

Of course! The servants would know something, regardless of the way they pretend to know nothing.

He hurried toward the bell and pulled on it with too much eagerness, nearly yanking it clear from its delicate string.

There was little else he could do for the time but wait for one of the waiters to appear.

In a surprisingly short time, there was a knock at the door, and he called out for the servant to enter.

"You rang, Your Grace?"

It was the same man he had seen with his wife in the lobby that very morning.

"What is your name?" James asked without preamble.

"Samuel, sir. Samuel Cassidy."

"Samuel, you know my wife, do you not? The Duchess of Holden?"

"Of course, sir." James noted a slight twitch in the maître d's cheek, but he dismissed it.

"And you must know my sister, Lady Elizabeth?"

"Yes, sir."

"Samuel, I must know how my sister fares."

Samuel's face remained stoic, unreadable.

"Sir? I am afraid I do not understand."

"You must know she is...unwell."

"No, sir, I know nothing of this."

James stifled a grunt.

"I will not tell a soul that you told me, Samuel, but this is a matter of much urgency."

"Forgive me, sir, but I know nothing on the matter."

James had no doubt that the man was lying, with his stormy eyes glittering as though he harbored a secret.

Yet there was no way to force the information from him. He likely feared for his job. After all, James was asking about the proprietor's daughter-in-law.

"Will you find my wife?" James asked, and an unmistakable brightness lit Samuel's eyes.

"Indeed, sir. Is there anything else?"

The same uncomfortable feeling that had crept over James that morning resurfaced in a flash. There was something that had troubled him about his wife speaking with Samuel although he could not possibly understand what.

She would never betray me with another and certainly not with a waiter.

"Sir?"

There was a rap on the door, and before he could respond, Lydia appeared, her face drawn.

"Lydia!" James sighed, hurrying toward her. "Is there any word?"

But Lydia's eyes widened, and she gasped when she noticed Samuel.

"Samuel!" she breathed. "What are you doing here?"

James froze and watched as the waiter and his wife exchanged a warm look, one which caused his stomach to clench.

"Your Grace," Samuel bowed in greeting. "I was called upon to search for you, but I can see now that I am no longer needed."

"No," James snapped, "you are not!"

Samuel bowed again and saw himself out, leaving the couple alone in James's chambers.

"What was the meaning of that?" James demanded when they were alone.

Lydia's eyes narrowed. "I have not a clue what you mean," she replied, but before he could explain his concern, she rushed on. "Would you or would you not like to know about Lise?"

"Of course," he cried, instantly ashamed that was not his first question. "Is she well?"

"She is still unconscious," Lydia explained. "But the midwife and Dr. Forrester did manage to deliver the child. They expect that Lise will recover, but she is very weak."

"I must see her," James cried, but Lydia shook her head.

"You cannot until she wakes and can attest that you did not put her into that state. Mr. Xavier is still beside himself with worry, and the child is quite small. It is not the time to cause more chaos among the Balfours."

"You cannot honestly expect me to remain here like a common criminal when I have done nothing wrong!"

"James, you must be patient. Dr. Forrester believes she will be awake soon, but there is far too much tension in the household as it is. Please, do not make this more trying of a time."

Her lovely face was rife with beseeching, and James knew he had no choice but to relent to her instructions.

"You will send for me the moment she wakes?" he sighed.

"Of course."

She turned to leave. James longed to call out, to ask her to stay, but something held him back.

It was not until she was gone that he realized what it was that had stopped him from asking her to remain. He had been terrified that Lydia would refuse.

9

The gardens outside were a splendid array of roses, snakeheads, and lilies of the valley. The aroma alone was enough to make a casual passerby believe they had crossed into paradise, but Lydia was unable to appreciate their beauty.

Her mind was a whirl, and her mother's endless chatter did nothing to alleviate the desolation growing within her.

"It does make more sense when you consider it," Elenora purred wickedly. "Who stood to gain from the late duke's death?"

"Mother, James did not murder his father," Lydia snapped, her wits at the end. "Would you kindly stop with such vicious speculation!"

"Do you not find it odd that half his family has befallen tragedy in such a short time? I would wager that the dowager duchess will, too, fall victim to foul play in the future if he continues to run amok."

"The late duke's death was an accident, and Lady Elizabeth was with child. The two incidences are completely unrelated to one another."

"So you say, child, but you are blinded by your affections for the monster."

"Mother, that is quite enough. You forget that you speak of my husband, the duke, no less."

"Which is why I have such valid concerns," Elenora insisted. "You cannot fault me for wanting to protect my child."

Does she ever truly think about my well-being or is that merely a fable she touts to enable her gossiping ways?

"I have been married to the duke for over three years. I daresay, if he was a monster, I would be privy to such information."

"Men can be very skilled liars when confronted, Lydia."

Lydia paused to stare at her mother with contempt.

"James is not a liar! He is not a killer, and he did not harm his sister, regardless of what Xavier Balfour might say in his grief. When Lady Elizabeth wakes, you will see how wrong you are, and I will smugly watch you choke on every one of the vile words you take so much relish in spewing forth."

She did not wait for her mother to recover from the cutting remarks. She scurried up the path toward the hotel through the servants' entrance even though she knew as a guest she was prohibited from using the door.

She did not care, her nerves far too raw for her to speak with another one of her peers until she regained her composure. The day had been long, not only with Lise's early labor but also the looks of thinly veiled contempt thrown her way by Xavier Balfour and his father. Elias had been the only man to offer her any semblance of comfort while the women were far too concerned about Lise's well-being to make comments on the situation.

All except her mother, of course. Elenora had commentary for every occasion.

Throughout the day, she had fought the urge to run back to James, who had seemed unusually compassionate toward her. When he had told her that he was ready to start their family, she was stunned at how apathetic the words had made her feel.

He is only saying this at the moment because he needs me. When we return to Holden, he will entrench himself in a dozen other tasks and forsake the idea.

She desperately wanted to believe him this time, but she had been disappointed far too many times in the past.

Even though he seemed so earnest, almost penitent.

"Your Grace, you should not be here."

She did not need to look up to know who it was that stood before her. Perhaps she had subconsciously gone there, hoping to see Samuel, shameful as it was.

"I understand," she murmured, turning to leave.

"Are you well, madam? May I get something for you?"

Tears of frustration filled her eyes, and she shook her head.

"No, Samuel, thank you. I only wished for a moment to gather my thoughts."

"Forgive me, madam. Of course, you are overwhelmed in the wake of Lady Elizabeth's condition. Do take all the time you require."

He turned to move away, but Lydia called out to him.

"Will you wait with me?" she breathed anxiously. "I-I do not feel much like being alone."

He stared at her pensively, sinking casually back against the wall.

"If you will forgive my boldness, madam, His Grace might appreciate your company also."

Lydia was mortified at the reminder.

"You need not stay, Samuel," she choked in humiliation. "Of course, I will see to my husband when I have word on his sister."

"I am happy to stay with you, madam," he replied quietly, but it did nothing to alleviate her embarrassment. She had misread his intentions, and she had never felt so foolish—or relieved.

She truly had no interest in this maître d', handsome as he might be. He had merely shown her some kindness, and she had immediately misinterpreted it.

"Forgive me, Samuel," she muttered, turning away as fat tears began to spill down her cheeks. "I fear I am terrible company at the moment."

"I fear you think that of yourself quite often, madam," Samuel told her, and she whipped her head back around.

"How would you know that?" she demanded, half awed, half alarmed at his astuteness.

"I have been many places, Your Grace, met many people, men, women, ladies, gentlemen..."

Once again, she wondered from where he hailed to have had such a colorful history, but she did not ask as she waited for him to finish his tale.

"You must understand, madam, that people are merely people, regardless of status, difficult as it must be for someone of your noble class to see."

"Of course, I realize that status has no bearing on our souls, Samuel," she replied, unsure if he was attempting to insult her. The intense warmth in his deep eyes told her that he was not.

"I have found that the worst pain that any living person can endure, the death of a loved one notwithstanding, is..."

He paused to ensure she was still listening.

"What is it?" she heard herself ask, leaning forward.

"Loneliness, madam."

Lydia wished she could feel defensive, argue with the idea, but even before she attempted, Samuel continued.

"There is quite a difference between being alone, Your Grace, and loneliness. One can be surrounded by many friends and kin but still feel a deep longing, a need to connect with another."

"W-why are you telling me this, Samuel?" she asked.

"Again, madam, if you will forgive my forwardness, I can sense the loneliness in others, which is why I am so drawn to you."

A wave of despair washed over her, and Lydia felt her lower lip quiver in denial, but she could not dispute what he was saying.

It was not attraction that pushed him toward me—it was pity.

She lowered her head, swallowing the lump in her throat as she shook her head.

"I do not need your attention, Samuel," she mumbled, turning toward the stairs. "Thank you."

She hurried away, sniffling back the upset that his words had caused, but simultaneously, she realized that she was oddly comforted by what had happened.

Something strange and wonderful had happened in the short time since she had come to the Balfour Hotel, something that gave her hope despite the turmoil occurring openly around her.

I am becoming more confident in myself. I would never have spoken to Mother like I did in the gardens nor would I have entertained the notion that another man found me comely before I came here.

"Your Grace! You should not be using these dark service stairs!" A young male waiter called.

Joshua, she remembered.

"I got quite turned around," she fibbed as Joshua hurried to escort her the rest of the way up the stairs toward the lobby.

"I suppose it is somewhat of a labyrinth to those who have not been born within these walls," Joshua jested, and Lydia found herself forming a bemused respect for the young man.

He is a boy, a servant, born into this life, and he smiles with a broad grin.

Yet she knew what it was—the hotel had a profound effect on all those who wandered through, regardless of how long they stayed. She truly believed it, as though God Himself had reached down to bless the hotel and the Balfours with a touch of his loving finger.

"Thank you, Joshua," Lydia said when he redirected her toward the main stairs off the lobby.

"It is a pleasure to have you here, Your Grace," Joshua offered happily before scampering off to complete his work. Lydia stared after him for a long while before mounting the stairs to the fifth floor.

To her surprise, no one lingered in the halls, but the door to Lise's quarters was ajar, and she heard the coo of a baby from within.

She raised her hand to knock and announce herself, but the sound of Xavier's voice stopped her from speaking.

"...are you certain?"

"Good Lord, Xavier," Lise snapped, her voice surprisingly strong. "How can you possibly think something so terrible. James is not my father."

Lydia's breath caught as she listened as the exchange continued.

"How would I know?" Xavier growled back. "I have only had one other occasion to have met him, and he was eager to defend your father at that time."

"James is in a difficult position," Lise sighed. "He is duke now. He could not jeopardize his relationship with my father at that time, but I assure you, he did not like what was happening when he was alive. James would never touch hide nor hair on me or Mother."

"Even if he suspected you murdered your father?"

Lydia's blood ran cold, and she willed herself to run away, to stop listening, but she could not, her curiosity overwhelming her wits.

Lise exhaled in a rush of wind.

"He would never believe that," she murmured. "We spoke about it. He was preparing to leave when this occurred..."

"What is it, my love?" Xavier asked, his voice hoarse with emotion. "What troubles you?"

"You know what," she replied quietly. "You know..."

"Lise, how many times must I assure you that I had nothing to do with his death."

"Shh!" she hissed. "He is falling asleep now."

"Forgive me," Xavier muttered. "But you infuriate me with this question. What makes you think that I would do anything so terrible?"

"Love," Lise answered gently. "I believe you would kill my father for love."

A combination of bitter and sweet showered down over Lydia as she backed out of their chambers, ashamed of herself for having eavesdropped.

Would I ever believe that James loved me enough to commit murder?

It was an atrocious thought, but not one she could easily shake. The late duke had been a beast, a cruel man who deserved nothing better than a painful death, but that did not make murder acceptable.

Still, there was a twisted romance to the devotion Xavier had toward his wife, one which Lydia wished for herself. She made her way toward her husband's rooms and entered without knocking, her mind twisted in confusion.

"Well?" James demanded, hurrying toward her. "Is she awake?"

He mistook her expression for one of disaster and paled instinctively.

"Oh, God..."

"She is awake, do not fret, but I have yet to see her. I do know that you are cleared of Mr. Xavier's accusations."

"Of course, I am," James laughed mirthlessly. "There was never any doubt in the matter."

She bit her lower lip and reached up to toy with the diamond brooch pinned to the neckline of her bodice.

"What is it, Lydia? What are you not telling me?" he demanded, his wry smile fading.

"Nothing!" she insisted. "You may go."

She waved him toward the door, but he did not move as he studied her face closely.

"Lydia," he insisted, "you are a terrible fibber. You always fiddle with your jewels when you have too many thoughts in your head."

"I do not...do I?"

She found herself oddly pleased that he noticed such a thing about her.

"You do, and you are contemplating something as we stand here. Please, Lydia, tell me."

If I tell him what I suspect, this will only fuel the quest he has sworn to leave behind. You need not tell him a thing, and we will return to Holden and forget this ever occurred.

The temptation was strong to walk away, but Lydia knew she could not do it in good conscience.

"James..." she began and he stared at her expectantly, the concern in his eyes apparent. "I believe your father was, indeed, murdered."

His mouth gaped.

"W-what? You have never spoken a word about this before. In fact, you have been deterred by all the gossip on the matter. Do not tell me your mother finally converted you into a believer!"

"No," Lydia drawled, biding her time. "Not my mother..."

"Lydia," there was impatience in his tone, "this has been a trying day for me also. Please, do come out with it."

"Your sister," she concluded. "Lise believes your father was murdered also...and that Xavier did it."

10

James found it impossible to look Xavier Balfour in the eye without his temper rising.

He realized that it had less to do with the idea that his brother-in-law had murdered his father and more to do with the fact that Xavier had attempted to lay blame upon James.

It was a clever ruse. Blame me, the son of an abusive brute, the one who stands to gain from my father's death, and the last one to be alone with Lise before the harrowing birth of her son.

"Your Grace, my wife does need her rest," Xavier told him gruffly. He had yet to apologize for his unjust accusations, but James was learning that his brother-in-law was not the most magnanimous fellow.

"I would just like to spend an extra moment with my nephew and sister," James countered, unmoving from Lise's bedside. "You do not mind if I remain another moment or two, do you, Lise?"

Lise looked at Xavier, who openly glared at James.

"Just another moment or two," she conceded and Xavier grunted.

"I will see to your dinner," he grumbled, storming from the room.

"You must forgive him, Jamie," his sister told him. "He loves me very much, and he worries terribly about my welfare in light of all that has happened."

"Did he kill Father, Lise?"

The directness of the question caused her visible shock, and she gasped, clutching her son closer to her chest in surprise.

"Of course not!" she sputtered. "Is this your scheme? To reverse the accusation he made in a moment of distress?"

"It is not a scheme, for I know you, too, believe he may have done it."

Lise's eyes widened to an almost unhealthy degree, and James wished he had not been so hard upon her.

"Never mind," he said, rising. "You must rest. I should not trouble you about this while you have endured so much."

"You should not trouble me at all!" she countered, her face flushing angrily. "Why can you not leave it well enough alone?"

He eyed her sadly.

"I have tried," he confessed, hanging his head. "But I feel as though his spirit filters through the halls of Pinehaven, demanding that I find his killer."

"Or perhaps you are merely feeling guilt for having claimed his title and are pursuing a ridiculous notion," Lise breathed. It was in that moment that James knew his fears were correct.

She believes it, too. Lydia was correct.

"Rest," James said again, shuffling toward the door. He paused to cast her a tight smile.

"I daresay, James is a potent name for a young lad."

Lise barely managed a smile, the stress on her face apparent.

"It is, is it not?"

"Good night, Lise. Rest well."

"Jamie...will you be leaving soon?"

He did not miss the anxious hope in her voice.

"Well, I would not leave when you are bedridden, Lise. What sort would I be to abandon my family at such a time?"

"Hm."

He could see she was not convinced in the least about his reasons but James did not care.

"Good night."

She did not respond as he made his way back into the hallway—where he ran directly into Elenora.

"Good evening, Lady Blackwell."

"It is a blessed evening, is it not?" Elenora conceded with a cheerfulness that James was not expecting. "I am pleased to know that your sister is well and the child is safe."

"God is merciful," James conceded, hoping to move past his mother-in-law. "You must forgive me, my lady, but I am expected somewhere."

It was untrue, of course, but he wanted to be anywhere else but with Elenora at that moment.

"Perhaps you should see about your wife," Elenora quipped with a smugness that turned James's blood cold.

"I intend to do precisely that—after I locate my mother."

"Your mother. I daresay, I have seen very little of her or Mrs. Anne Balfour since we arrived."

"Perhaps that is because they are avoiding your rather shrewd tongue, Lady Blackwell."

The smirk froze on Elenora's face.

"Some ladies are less welcoming of the truth than others."

"And what truth might that be, my lady? The truth that my mother murdered my father or the truth that I did?"

Her smile faded away completely now, and Elenora scowled deeply.

"We all know your father fell unnaturally."

"As you say, Lady Blackwell. If you will excuse me."

"When will we leave this God-forsaken place?" Elenora cried after him. "I was promised we would go as soon as your sister was well."

James did not answer, but he strode down the stairs purposefully, his breaths escaping in short, angry rasps.

"Your Grace!" Byron whispered in a staged way. "What a pleasant surprise!"

"Byron, you must arrange for a coach to leave directly on the morrow, as early as possible."

He nodded. "Will you be leaving, sir?"

"No," James replied flatly. "Lady Blackwell will be returning to Whittaker."

"Do you mean Holden, sir?"

"No," James said through clenched teeth. "I mean Whittaker."

"Very good, sir. I will arrange it at once. Is that all, Your Grace?"

James studied him. "I do not know, Byron. Is that all?"

The concierge seemed somewhat flustered by the query. "I-I am unsure, sir. Is there another matter in which I can assist you?"

"Last night, Byron, you seemed quite prepared to tell me something, but we were interrupted. What was it you meant to say?"

Byron balked and looked away.

"No, Your Grace, you are mistaken. I only wished to extend my condolences to your family. I-I was here at the time the news was received, and I did feel quite badly for Lady Elizabeth."

"Are you sure, Byron for if there is something you would like me to know, I am listening with an open heart and mind."

Byron dropped his eyes fully and seemed to be contemplating his next words carefully. "I was here that night," Byron offered in a barely audible voice. "It was a strange evening, like ghosts were wandering through the halls."

"Ghosts? How so?"

"Doors were opening and closing, unlocking on their own, and it was so quiet on the family's floor."

James managed to keep his face impassive although he was beginning to wonder if the old man was of sound enough mind to know what he recalled.

"The family's floor? The fifth floor?"

"Indeed."

"I thought that Mr. Balfour had gone out on business...but at that hour of the night?"

"What hour?" James demanded, leaning across the desk. "What hour of the night?"

"I daresay Joshua saw the same ghost at two of the morning."

"Joshua?"

"The young waiter. He was born here, sir, second-generation Balfour. A good lad, honest."

"I know him," James said, his mind racing.

"Alas, it could not have been Mr. Balfour," Byron continued. "He was here at dawn, well rested. No one returned that night, but the guard came on the morrow to announce the duke's passing. I could not help but wonder if the duke himself was not haunting the halls, looking for his wife and daughter to bid them goodbye."

Excitement coursed through James, and it took all he had to contain himself.

"Thank you, Byron," he said, maintaining his nonchalance. "You have been most helpful."

"Have I?" Byron asked sadly. "Why do I feel as though I have merely awoken a sleeping spirit?"

But James was barely listening.

"You will not forget that coach for the morrow?"

"No, sir, of course not. Good night."

"Good night," James muttered, turning away.

Someone in the hotel, someone on the family's floor disappeared the night my father passed. Could it have been Xavier?

Blood rushed through his veins like a waterfall as he hurried toward the staff's quarters.

He needed to speak with Joshua immediately.

∽

To HIS GREAT RELIEF, Joshua worked the night shift, and James found the young man dismantling the dining hall.

"Joshua," he called, and the boy raised his head, an instant smile upon his face.

"Your Grace! How may I assist you?"

"I have a rather odd question for you," he replied slowly.

"Those are the best kinds, sir."

The boy straightened to his full, gangly height and peered at James with inquisitive eyes.

"Do you recall a rather peculiar evening, several months ago in the winter when you saw a ghost?"

Joshua chuckled but immediately stopped when he saw the expression on James's face. "Oh! Pardon me, sir. A ghost you say?"

"I should have used better phrasing," James offered sheepishly. "It would have been a night when you and Byron thought you saw someone leaving the hotel before the witching hour."

"Oh." Understanding lit Joshua's bright eyes. "Certainly, Your Grace. That was the night your father passed, was it not?"

James blinked at the boy, stunned by his memory.

"Indeed, it was," he replied slowly. "You have quite a healthy mind, Joshua."

The boy shrugged humbly.

"I attempt to keep sharp when possible," he chuckled, looking about the dark dining hall.

A few candelabra held lit candles to cast shadows along the walls in eerie shapes.

"Unfortunately, I do not see a great deal of excitement so I tend to recall when something of substance occurs."

"What made it so memorable?" James demanded, his pulse quickening. "What did you see?"

"I fear I cannot tell you much, Your Grace, for I only thought I saw the specter of someone leaving through the front doors. Of course, only the family would have keys to permit themselves to leave—assuming Byron locked the doors at all when he went on his rounds of the building."

"Has he a history of forgetfulness?"

"No..." Joshua murmured, seeming uncomfortable. "But I daresay —and with all the respect due to him—that he is a man in his sixties. He should not be working."

Shame lit Joshua's face. "Please do not tell him I said such a thing. He is a decent, dear man who—"

James held up his hand and shook his head. "I assure you, I will tell him nothing, but you must remember harder. Tell me about this specter. What of him?"

Joshua shook his head and stared down at his well-polished shoes.

"If you will forgive me, sir, I cannot be sure it was a 'he' at all."

James blinked in confusion.

"Surely, you do not truly believe you saw a ghost, Joshua."

He laughed nervously. "No, sir, not a ghost...but a woman."

James's mouth parted as he tried to reconcile this new revelation.

"A woman? A guest perhaps?"

"Truthfully, Your Grace, I had not given it much thought. If Byron had left the doors unlocked, perhaps it was merely one of the guests."

Yet if Byron locked the doors, it would have to have been a woman. Emmeline? Or could he have mistaken Xavier for a woman?

That was highly unlikely. Xavier was far too tall and muscular to ever have been construed as a woman.

Unless he was in a disguise...

None of this made a lick of sense to James, and he was beginning to think he was merely wasting his time.

"I see I have not been remotely helpful, Your Grace."

"You have," James assured him, flashing a quick smile. "I am sorry to have interrupted your work."

"I welcome the break from the monotony," Joshua replied, returning his grin. "However, I do not believe the Balfours feel the same."

"Then, I will not keep you. Good night."

"Good night, Your Grace."

With a disappointed sigh, James left the dining room.

Perhaps he had not found the answers he sought, but he felt as though he was getting closer. There was nothing else he could do that night, but perhaps the morning light would provide him with a clearer head.

All he wished to do at that moment was find his wife and ask her to join him for a nightcap before retiring for the night.

And on the morrow, after I send Elenora far away from us both, I will turn in the key to Lydia's suite so that she will sleep beside me where she belongs.

With a renewed sense of faith, James hurried up the stairs to find his wife, a mounting sense of expectation rising within him, like he was a young man, courting for the first time.

It is not unlike courting, he realized. *We have been little other than two strangers living beneath the same roof for several years. I have been the daft fool who has overlooked Lydia's grace and beauty while she has been vying for my attention. I do not deserve her. I am blessed to have her.*

He paused outside her bedchambers and looked about with some helplessness. He wished he had at least a flower to present to her.

Idly, he considered retreating to the gardens, but a quick look at his pocket watch told him that Lydia would most certainly be asleep by the time he returned. She had been run ragged throughout the day. He might not find her awake even now.

"Lydia?" he called, gently rapping on the door. "Are you present?"

There was no response from inside, and given the hour, he did not dare knock louder, but when he tried the handle, it gave way easily, and he stepped inside the purely dark suite.

"Lydia?" he whispered. "Are you asleep?"

He listened for signs of her breathing, but as he neared her bed, he could clearly see the bed fully made by the light of the moon through the open drapes.

"Lydia?"

His confusion turned to anger as he lit a candle and searched the room for signs of his wife, but she simply was not there.

Dread rose in his gut as he thought of the way the maître d' had looked at her earlier, and a sick feeling overtook him.

With a heavy heart, he sank onto the bed, his throat thick with bile.

I lost her before I ever had a chance to make matters right between us —and I have no one to blame but myself.

11

The light of the moon never ceased to capture her heart, as if a part of Lydia lived somewhere in the heavens above. She had not even attempted to sleep, knowing that the endless jumble of thoughts in her mind would keep her up for yet another night. Lydia should have been exhausted, and while she felt a certain fatigue inside, it was not unlike the one she had known since her marriage to James had commenced.

You should not have told him what you heard. Perhaps Mr. Xavier murdered the duke or perhaps not. James was ready to leave it be and you only brought it forward again, creating more doubt, more problems, more questions.

She trailed her fingers along the wrought iron as she continued to walk beneath the rays of the half moon, her heart heavying with each step. She knew much better than to be wandering about unchaperoned and alone at night, but it was something she had done since she was a child. It gave her a sense of peace, being completely shrouded from prying eyes and ears, even if it was terribly scandalous. She had never been caught in the past, and eventually, Lydia forgot that it was an issue at all.

She was alone with her dismal, gray thoughts, the very same way she had been since girlhood.

It will never be over, she thought with some sadness. *If he is not chasing ghosts, he will be busy with matters of the duchy. I will never be as important to James as Emmeline is to Elias or Lise is to Xavier. I must accept that.*

She did not know why it was becoming such a devastating realization suddenly. She had always known it. She supposed being in the presence of true love had made Lydia long for what she had never had.

Up ahead, she saw movement against the stone path, and she reeled back, ducking into the bushes.

Oh! I have been caught walking about unescorted! James will be furious with me when this is discovered.

"Your Grace?"

Lydia was mortified.

"Your Grace, is that you?"

She knew she had been caught.

By Samuel no less!

"Yes, Samuel," she muttered guiltily, stepping from the bed of thorns to face him with some shame.

"A-are you alone?" he demanded, looking about in shock. "W-where is your chaperone?"

"I seem to have lost her," Lydia replied. "I will return to the hotel and find her."

"I will see you back…" Samuel offered, but he seemed uncomfortable by the idea, and Lydia knew precisely why. If they were seen together, he would most certainly be terminated on the spot.

"You need not," Lydia told him quickly. "I assure you, my hand-maiden is about."

She pretended to look about, but Samuel did not look convinced.

"Your Grace, a lady of your status cannot simply wander the grounds on her own. If any misfortune were to befall you…"

He extended his arm for her accept.

"I realize this is not the dandiest arm in Luton, but I hope it will suffice."

"Samuel, I vow to run back to the hotel before anyone is any wiser about my absence."

"Of course, you do not need to take my arm," he continued as though she had not spoken, "and we can simply walk side by side."

He started forward, pausing after a few steps to glance at her.

"Shall we?"

Lydia was incensed with herself for putting this man in such a position. She vowed that would be the last walk she ever took alone unchaperoned, and she reached for his arm as they continued up the path.

"What brings you out at this hour of the night?"

"I was on my way to Luton when I saw you moving about in the bushes. I thought I might investigate, lest you were a wolf."

"A wolf?" Lydia laughed. "And how would you go about disabling a wolf if I had been one?"

"I am much faster than I appear, Your Grace," Samuel chuckled.

"I should hope so if you expect to defend yourself against a wolf." They stopped a moment, and Lydia peered up at him regretfully. "I am sorry I have ruined your night."

"Ruined?" Samuel echoed. "Luton never sleeps, Madam, quite like yourself, it appears."

Again, Lydia giggled.

"I suspect I have too much on my mind," she sighed as they continued toward the hotel. Once more, she paused and stared at him with a fragile smile on her face.

"I would also like to apologize for being so rude this afternoon. Your words reached me deeply, and I fear I acted quite foolishly."

"You did nothing wrong, madam. There is no need for an apology."

Their eyes met and smiles widened.

"I—"

"Unhand her!"

Lydia spun about, her skirts sweeping along the pathway as her eyes sought to find James in the darkness until suddenly, he loomed above her, raging with anger and distress.

"Your Grace, i-it is not what it seems," Samuel muttered and even in the low light, Lydia could see his bronze skin wan.

"A likely story!" James hissed, advancing upon him. "Have you no shame? She is a duchess! You are a common—"

"James, that is quite enough!" Lydia snapped furiously. "Samuel found me alone in the gardens. He was merely seeing me back to the hotel."

James eyed her skeptically.

"Why would you be alone in the gardens?"

"It is simply something I do on occasion," she muttered, darting her eyes away in shame. "Run along now, Samuel. Luton awaits."

Samuel remained in place, waiting for the duke to confirm her instructions.

"Is this true?"

"It is, Your Grace," Samuel sighed. "Please, I understand how this must seem to you, but I assure you, I would never dishonor you in such a way."

"Nor would I, James," Lydia sighed. "Do not fault the man. He was only doing what he thought was right."

James met her eyes, his face contorting in perplexity.

"Permit him to go, James," Lydia insisted, and slowly, James turned back to nod curtly at Samuel.

"Go," he barked, and Samuel scampered off, bowing as he muttered his gratitude. As he disappeared into the darkness, James turned his attention back toward her.

"It was foolish," she conceded before he could even speak. "I will not go out without a chaperone again."

James no longer looked angry, but ashamed and flustered.

"I-I thought you had taken him as a lover."

The pain in his voice was almost palpable, and Lydia frowned, her cheeks flushing as she remembered how she had thought about Samuel the previous evening.

How greatly everything can change in one day, she thought with some bemusement. *James has gained a new nephew and I have lost my sacred walks alone.*

"I would never dishonor myself nor you by taking on a lover," Lydia told him flatly. "I should not need to tell you that."

"I know. You are good, decent, and kind. You have been by my side when I did not deserve you. I thought you had taken a lover, and my world fell into a thousand pieces around me."

Lydia's jaw fell at her husband's unexpected words.

"Forgive me, Lydia, for overlooking your wonder, your grace. Forgive me for putting you last when I should have always put you first. If you will permit me, I will spend my life making you see that I do love you. I always have."

Tears sprang to her eyes, and she nodded, reaching for his hands. Their bodies drew nearer, and Lydia caught the glint of the moon reflecting in his eyes.

"I cannot tell you how long I have yearned to hear those words," she confessed, a sob choking her voice slightly.

"I am ashamed that I have left you yearning for something you very much deserve, my wife. I assure you, you will hear them with greater frequency," he promised, placing a soft kiss against her lips. His touch sent waves of warmth spiraling through her body, and abruptly, all the tension she had felt building in her shoulders melted away into nothing but a glorious flutter of love.

"Are you well?" he asked, peering down at her face, and Lydia smiled sleepily.

"Yes," she murmured. "I am very well."

"Then, I suggest we return to the hotel and put you to rest."

～

LYDIA SLEPT WELL for the first time in as long as she could recall, her dreams leaving her refreshed and contented when she awoke. James was still at her side, staring lovingly at her face when her eyes fluttered open.

"Good morning," her husband murmured, and Lydia was over-come with adoration.

"Have you been watching me as I slumbered?" she asked, slightly abashed.

"I have. Does that embarrass you?"

Lydia sat up and shook her head slightly, although her cheeks blushed a deep rose. It would take some time to become accustomed to this newfound attention, but she did not dislike it.

"When you are prepared," James continued, "I would hope you would dress and see me to a rather unpleasant task this day."

The soft smile faded from Lydia's lips, and she watched him with wary speculation. "What might that be?" she asked, wishing he had allowed her only a few more moments of oblivious peace.

"You must not be upset. It is for the best," he told her, a slightly concerned look upon his face and she tensed, sitting up against the sheets.

"James..."

"I have arranged for your mother to be on the first coach back to Whittaker this morning."

Lydia blinked and stared at him in disbelief, a swirl of emotions accompanying the announcement.

"Will I be with her?" Lydia asked, her voice hoarse with disap-pointment.

Is that why he has been so kind to me? He intends to see me off and out of his way?

"Of course not!" James cried, appearing shaken that she had even suggested such a thing. "I thought I made my position quite clear last night. You belong at my side. Your mother belongs in Whittaker. Her endless meddling has not helped our marriage any more than my endless obsessions. It is high time we eliminate the outside influ-ences and focus the attention due on ourselves."

Lydia's heart swelled with affection and hope as she stared at him.

Mother will be incensed when she hears of this, she thought, but it did not trouble her in the least. There would most certainly be an after-math with which to deal, but for the first time, Lydia felt a confidence in her husband, in their union, and the direction in which it was going.

"Are you distraught?" James asked, mistaking her silence for upset.

"No," she denied, slipping her legs over the side of the bed to rise. "Well, yes."

She paused to glance at him, and James's brow furrowed. He exhaled slowly and met her gaze.

"I realize she is your mother, Lydia, but she has caused nothing but grief since her arrival. Her presence only serves to hinder us. I know she is not solely to blame for all that has happened between us, but she does not help."

Lydia slowly padded around the bed, her nightgown flowing loosely about her as she neared him, a gentle smile on her face.

"You misunderstand me," she murmured, placing her palms on his face to peer into his eyes. "I am not distraught at you."

"Oh?"

She shook her head, her smile widening slightly.

"I am merely distraught that I did not consider it first," she confessed, and relief crossed James's face.

He laughed merrily and embraced her, burying his face against the cotton of her gown before releasing a deep sigh.

"I have failed you in so many ways, Lydia," he sighed. "But I swear I will not permit it to happen again."

Lydia nodded slowly, her hands lacing through his thick hair to stroke him lovingly.

"I have faith in us," she whispered, and she realized it was so. She had clung to the hope that one day her husband would see the love he had waiting for him, and that day had finally come.

Not another word was exchanged as a loud, irritable voice cried out from the hall beyond their rooms, and Lydia disentangled herself from James's hold. She had no doubt who was causing the commotion at such an early hour.

"It seems that Mother has discovered her fate," she muttered and James snorted.

"We best tend to her before she wakes the entire hotel."

"It is likely too late for that," Lydia sighed, but she did not move, her gaze fixed on James. There was suddenly no urgency, no need to rush about or hide or flee. James was on her side, wholly and completely.

The rest of the world could wait.

12

❧❧❧

Sending Elenora off proved to be a bigger chore than James had anticipated. She had fought like a caged tiger, shouting in an unladylike fashion, threatening reprisal. The other guests watched in shock as she was herded into the waiting coach.

"Forgive the display," James muttered to the Balfours after the carriage finally moved away. "She is quite unaccustomed to being told no."

Charlton snickered.

"I have a wife not unlike that," he muttered. "Excuse me. I have matters to attend in the office."

He sauntered back inside the hotel, leaving James and Lydia outside to contemplate their future.

"What will we do now?" Lydia asked quietly when the coach had all but disappeared. "Will we return to Holden?"

James was silent for a long moment. It was the proper thing to do, take his wife home and start anew with all the chaos of the past few days behind them.

That is certainly what she deserves, and I have sacrificed enough time away from her.

"Yes," he told her, managing to keep the reluctance from his tone.

"I will bid my sister adieu, and we will make arrangements to leave at once."

Lydia's arm tightened against his, and her fingers moved to twirl at the pearls encircling her neck.

"What is it, my love?" he asked gently. "You do not wish to leave?"

She eyed him through her peripheral gaze before releasing a sigh.

"I do rather enjoy it here," she confessed. "There is a certain tranquility to be found."

"We might remain for a few more days," he agreed.

"Moreover, you have not yet learned who killed your father."

James's mouth firmed, and he shook his head with vehemence.

"I have decided to forsake that quest," he told her. "That has consumed far too much of my thoughts and for what?"

"For your peace of mind, darling."

She turned to look at her husband with compassionate eyes.

"You will never fully rest until you know for certain, James, and I was wrong to expect you to leave it alone."

"You have always supported me, Lydia."

"Not enough," she insisted. "I have done little to assist you in finding the truth about what happened that night. I pledge myself to you now. We will determine the truth before we leave here."

How am I so blessed? He asked himself yet again.

"I fear that this is a matter that might never be resolved," he said softly, making his decision. "I do not wish to pursue it for another moment, Lydia. You and I have much lost time for which to compensate. We will put the unpleasantness of my father's death in the past where it belongs. We might stay a few more days, but then we will return to Holden and never speak of the matter again."

He did not miss the glint of hope that sprang into her kind eyes.

"As you wish, my husband," she murmured, curling her fingers into his arm. "We shall call this the honeymoon we never had."

"Indeed," he agreed, wrapping his own gloved hand around hers. "Consider us newly wed."

∾

THE NEXT FEW days took on a very different tone. Elenora's absence seemed to lift a weight off Lydia's shoulders, and James noticed with deep contentment that his wife was truly resplendent in her happiness.

Lydia spent her days with Emmeline Compton, who seemed delighted to have a new companion while James grew to know his brother-in-law.

Despite their initial impression of one another, James found himself warming to the man. They both loved Lise, after all, and as Xavier realized James was not there to stir trouble any longer, the proprietor's son slowly welcomed him into the fold.

Their dinners were pleasant, although James still had yet to spend time alone with his mother. It was becoming more and more apparent to him that Patience was deliberately avoiding him, often running off to hide in Anne Balfour's suite before James could find her. On the third night of again missing his opportunity, he saw Lydia to their chambers and told her of his plan.

"I cannot leave here tomorrow without speaking to my mother," he told Lydia. "I must at the very least apologize for the way I took her unawares by coming here. I had hoped she would have accepted by now that we mean her no harm."

"You do as you must," Lydia told him gently. "It would be a shame to return to Holden knowing that she did not feel welcome to return also."

With relief, he placed a gentle kiss on her rouged cheek.

"I shall not be long," he promised. "Will you attempt to wait for me?"

"Of course," Lydia agreed, serving him a warm smile. "I would like to know what she says."

James took a full breath and hurried from their chambers toward his mother's room, where he knocked softly. The hour was early enough, and to his great surprise, Patience called out for him to enter.

"Oh," she choked when she saw her son. "James."

"Mother, please do not send me on my way," he pleaded. "I am not here to cause you any discomfort."

Patience's eyes darted toward the doorway.

"I-I had been expecting a waiter," she muttered, and James realized that was the only reason she had permitted him entry.

"Mother, if you will simply hear me out, I will be on my way."

Patience cast him a nervous look and rose from the vanity to wrap her dressing robe about her body as she approached him in the sitting room.

"I would never send you away, Jamie. You are my son."

"Lydia and I will be leaving tomorrow," he explained to her as she cautiously neared him. "Before we do, I want to be sure that we are at peace, Mother. Whatever Lady Blackwell said that first night—that is not my belief."

"Do not fib to your mother, Jamie. Of course, you believed I had a hand in Edward's death. You would not have come otherwise."

A flush of embarrassment tinged his cheeks, and James lowered his eyes.

"It was wrong to have come here in such a manner. I assure you, Mother, I do not think you are to blame."

Patience's eyes narrowed, her face paling slightly.

"Have you moved on to another suspect, then?"

"I-no, Mother. I will stop with this madness. Nothing good can come out of it."

Patience did not forsake the look of skepticism.

"What do you know about that night, Jamie?" she asked. "What have you gleaned?"

A fission of alarm snaked through his veins as he stared at his mother's face. What he saw there caused all his doubts to flood back in a torrent.

She knows something about what became of father!

He willed himself not to consider it, to leave the terrible ordeal behind him as he had promised Lydia he would, but his mother's eyes bore into him with intensity.

"You must tell me, Jamie," she hissed with some urgency. "What have you learned?"

"What do you know, Mother?" he countered, his blood racing. "You know what happened that night."

Mother and son continued to stare at one another for long moments, neither willing to falter, but in the end, it was Patience who looked away.

"Close the door," she murmured. "And I will tell you all I know."

His heart leaped into his throat as he hurried to oblige her request. Could this be a ruse, a way to deter him from looking into this further?

Tell her you do not want to know, a small voice cried out to him. *Tell her that it does not matter.*

Yet he did none of that. Instead, he sat gingerly on the edge of the settee as Patience did the same, again locking eyes with her son.

"I do not need to tell you what your father did to me, to your sister," his mother began.

"You do not, Mother," James mumbled. "I should have done much more to protect you."

"It is not your duty to protect your mother from your father," Patience corrected him. "It is a mother's duty to shelter her children, however, and that was what I tried to do with Lise."

"No one faults you for what you did," James agreed. "You had no choice."

"Bringing Lise here was the best move I could have ever made for both her and myself, even if I did not realize it at the time," Patience sighed, sinking back, a faraway look in her eyes. "Lise found love with Xavier—love, security, and a family. I, too, found security and friendship in the most unlikely place."

"Anne Balfour?" James guessed, and as he said the name, a burning sensation filled his head.

Anne Balfour.

"She is a troubled soul," Patience continued, her eyes glazed. "But she was always my friend, and no one was more devastated by us running off than Anne."

"Oh, Mother..." Bile rose in the back of James's throat.

Anne Balfour. A woman with a key to the front doors. No one would

have noticed if she was not about in the morning. She had every opportu-
nity to leave the hotel.

"She is not of completely sound mind, Jamie, but her intentions were pure. She blamed your father for us leaving, and she was right, in a way. We never could have returned if he remained alive."

James did not know what to say, and he swallowed the misery bubbling up from his stomach.

"She is not a murderess," Patience muttered. "Although, you might not see it that way. If she had not done what she did, your sister and I would likely be dead ourselves. Not to mention your nephew."

James ground his teeth together and held back the rush of words that threatened to spill forward.

"You may do what you must, James, but there is not an iota of proof, and if I am asked again, I will deny that I ever told you."

"Why are you telling me?" James finally managed to sputter. "Why now?"

Patience's expression filled with sympathy and she sighed heavily.

"Because despite all that your father was, he was still your father, and I know you, Jamie. You will go to your grave wondering what happened, regardless of what you say. You deserve the truth. What you do with that truth is yours to decide."

James rose numbly, and there was a sharp knock on the door.

"Who is there?" Patience called tensely.

"Samuel, Your Grace."

His mother nodded at James before calling out for Samuel to enter.

"Oh, forgive me," Samuel muttered. "I did not realize you had company, madam. Good evening, Your Grace."

"Samuel," James muttered. "I was just leaving."

"James," Patience called out as he stumbled toward the door, the news sitting like a rock in his gut. James could not bring himself to stop and look his mother in the eye.

He made his way back toward his chambers and stood there for a long moment, collecting his thoughts and willing his heart rate to return to normal.

Anne Balfour is a drunk. A lonely, pitiful drunk with a family who will be destroyed by this revelation.

He thought of his sister, of the love she had found in Xavier Balfour, of his frail baby nephew. James considered the peace that Lydia had found at the hotel and the way he had been reunited with his wife.

James drew back his shoulders and entered the bedchambers, his face stoic. Lydia sat reading on the chaise, her long hair loose around her shoulders.

"You have returned so soon?" she asked, setting the novel aside to hurry toward him. "Is all well?"

He studied her face closely, imagining how much more devastation he would cause if he told her what he had learned.

No, he vowed. *I made a promise to her to leave this matter alone and I will honor it. I owe this much to my wife.*

"Darling? What is the matter?" Lydia breathed, her words laced with concern.

"Not a thing," he replied, pulling her close into his embrace. "Everything is precisely as it should be."

EPILOGUE

S now fell in a nearly twisting, twirling dance as Lydia rushed toward the approaching messenger.

"Your Grace! Permit me to go," Franny called from the threshold, but Lydia paid her no mind as the messenger's horse stopped.

"I seek the Duke of Holden," the page explained.

"I am the duchess," Lydia replied, reaching eagerly for the message. She knew what it contained, and her excitement was close to bubbling over.

"I have an invitation from the Balfour Hotel in Luton," the young man continued.

"I am aware," Lydia replied impatiently. "Do give it to me."

He handed her the creamy paper, and Lydia spun back toward the manor house, shivering as she crossed the threshold.

"Your Grace, you will catch your death running outside without a cloak," Franny chided in her motherly way.

"I am fit as a fiddle," Lydia assured her, opening the page with trembling fingers.

"What is this I hear?" James demanded, appearing in the entry-way. "Have you been running into the snow?"

"It is here," Lydia breathed, waving the paper before him while ignoring his question. "The invitation has arrived!"

James laughed gently and took her arm, leading her toward the crackling warmth of the fireplace inside the front salon.

"As we knew it would be," he conceded. "I daresay, my duchess, I have never seen a lady quite so excited to attend a christening in all my life."

"You know as well as I do, my love, that I have every cause to be elated. We are to be his godparents!"

James offered her another warm smile, and Lydia stared at him.

"Why are you not more excited?" she demanded. "This will be wonderful..."

Her brow furrowed slightly.

"Are you concerned about seeing your mother and sister again?"

"No," he denied quickly. "Not in the least. I am pleased that we are returning to Luton. I suspect that you miss Emmeline Compton more than you confess."

"I do," Lydia agreed. "But as you continue to remind me, I am free to visit at any time. She warns me that there is little to do in the winter months, however."

Lydia continued to gaze at him. "What is the matter, Your Grace?"

James again shook his head and turned away, causing a familiar sense of alarm in Lydia's gut. She could not say why, but since they had come back from Luton after those enlightening few days in the summer months, Lydia could not help but feel that her husband had returned with a secret.

The matter of his father never again was roused, and sometimes she wondered if he was still thinking about it. Whenever she broached the topic, however, he dismissed it with a wave.

"There is nothing on my mind but you and the duchy," he would assure her, and Lydia would have no other option but to accept his word.

"James, would you rather we not go to Luton for the christening?" Lydia asked nervously. She dreaded that he might refuse the invitation, but to her relief, he laughed.

"I would not dare suggest such a thing," he replied. "I am rather looking forward to the trip."

"Then, what is it? Do not say it is nothing when I can clearly see you are somewhere else in thought."

His mouth puckered, and James released a slow groan. "Must you know me so well?" he sighed.

"I can think of worse things to complain about than your wife being familiar with your moods."

"It is not a mood," James insisted, turning back to look at her, a glass of scotch in hand. "I was simply considering that Lise named the baby after me."

"That should flatter you, not trouble you," Lydia chuckled. "My word, you are the most complicated gentleman in the land."

James's smile broadened. He shook his head, gently placing his drink to the side as he neared her.

"I am flattered," he replied, chuckling. "In fact, I suggested that she name the child after me. Of course, I did not think she actually would."

"She loves you a great deal more than you might think," Lydia said softly. "I am happy you have reconciled with her."

"Our family is blessed with togetherness," he agreed but the shadow did not pass from his eyes.

"What is it, then?" Lydia urged, with a growing feeling of uneasiness. "Please, James, you must not have me guess."

"I was merely thinking about what we will do if our child is a boy," he muttered. "Will we name him James also?"

Lydia gaped at him in shock.

"H-how did you know?" she breathed. "I-I only just learned myself."

James blinked at her uncomprehendingly. "About what?"

"T-that I am with child..."

His eyes bugged almost clear from their sockets as he stared at her.

"Are you?" he gasped, and Lydia was terribly embarrassed. She had planned to tell him in a much more intimate manner, but the secret was out now.

"I am," she murmured. "We will finally have the family I have always longed for."

Tears of joy filled her eyes, and James embraced her gently.

"Indeed," he agreed. "He will want for nothing, our son."

"The baby marquis."

They parted to stare at one another.

"We will keep this news to ourselves until after the christening," Lydia told him and James agreed. His brow creased.

"What is it now?"

"It is the same matter," James moaned. "What will we name the baby marquis?"

Lydia laughed, knowing her husband merely jested.

"James," she replied. "We will name him James as well."

~

NEXT BOOK: Her Scandalously Entangled Heart

I'd like to thank you for reading this book. I hope you enjoyed it.

Please view my other titles at:
https://books2read.com/amandadavis

Printed in Great Britain
by Amazon